SWEET TOOTH AND OTHER STORIES

SWEET TOOTH AND OTHER STORIES

SERKAN GÖRKEMLI

UNIVERSITY PRESS OF KENTUCKY

Scholarly publisher for the Commonwealth, serving Bellarmine University, Berea College, Centre College of Kentucky, Eastern Kentucky University, The Filson Historical Society, Georgetown College, Kentucky Historical Society, Kentucky State University, Morehead State University, Murray State University, Northern Kentucky University, Spalding University, Transylvania University, University of Kentucky, University of Louisville, University of Pikeville, and Western Kentucky University.
All rights reserved.

Editorial and Sales Offices: The University Press of Kentucky
663 South Limestone Street, Lexington, Kentucky 40508-4008
www.kentuckypress.com

A note to the reader: This book contains sensitive material, including several depictions of characters using homophobic language. Discretion is advised.

Library of Congress Cataloging-in-Publication Data

Names: Görkemli, Serkan, author.
Title: Sweet tooth and other stories / Serkan Görkemli.
Description: Lexington, Kentucky : University Press of Kentucky, 2024. | Series: University press of Kentucky new poetry & prose
Identifiers: LCCN 2023051402 (print) | LCCN 2023051403 (ebook) | ISBN 9781985900196 (cloth ; acid-free paper) | ISBN 9781985900202 (paperback ; acid-free paper) | ISBN 9781985900226 (adobe pdf) | ISBN 9781985900219 (epub)
Subjects: LCGFT: Short stories.
Classification: LCC PS3607.O5976 S94 2024 (print) | LCC PS3607.O5976 (ebook) | DDC 813/.6—dc23/eng/20231212
LC record available at https://lccn.loc.gov/2023051402
LC ebook record available at https://lccn.loc.gov/2023051403

For my family

CONTENTS

WEBBED

Eleven-year-old Hasan contemplated his left hand. They were wheeling him on a gurney through the corridors of the state hospital in Çorlu in 1989. He was to undergo a surgery to remove the webbing between his ring and middle fingers so that—his parents told him—he could wear a wedding ring when he got married one day.

The scent of bleach emanated from the floors. The whitewashed walls had occasional ghostly smudges from hands and fingers. A framed black-and-white photograph of a nurse shushed everyone with her index finger pressed against her lips. Another frame showed Mustafa Kemal Atatürk, the founding father of the Republic, whose images, accompanied with his signature in cursive, graced all government offices, classrooms at Hasan's school, and wall calendars at homes, the ubiquitous reminders of the nation's love affair with a man who had passed fifty-one years ago.

The corridors were lined with benches that sagged under the weight of the sick who had waited since dawn for their turn to see overwhelmed doctors. Occasional coughs came from different directions. Some heads, eyes closed, rested against the walls; others were cradled on one side by palms that partially covered sleepy or worried eyes. Having finally secured a place in the long line to see the doctor, others were awake; they stirred hot black tea as they munched on their makeshift breakfasts of savory *simit* or warm *poğaça*. Hasan inhaled and felt his stomach drop.

They gave him a little white pill—to calm him down, they said. Next, they asked him to change into a hospital gown and put on a surgical cap. The cap reminded him of when he was four or five and had long, wispy hair. His parents wanted to have it cut short, despite his protests; they said he would otherwise be mistaken for a girl, which had happened a few times. Each time, they corrected the offender, grabbed Hasan's hand, and walked away, heads high.

As ethnic Turks, they had immigrated a few years ago to the motherland from Bulgaria to escape communist assimilation campaigns. In the post-coup 1980s, their desire to fit in, their newfound need to reclaim their ancestral Turkishness, exacted a self-surveillance that neutralized any difference perceived to be un-Turkish. They were bilingual yet no longer spoke Bulgarian, and they forbade Hasan from doing so. They started observing Muslim holidays with more passion than usual, to find common ground with other Turks, and talked about sending Hasan to the Koran school at the local mosque during summer break.

When Hasan started elementary school, his father took him to a barbershop, where they seated children on a wooden board placed on the armrests of the barber's chair. Elevated, he watched his reflection in the mirror. Covered in a black apron pinned around his neck, he shed tears quietly while his father frowned over the sports section of *Hürriyet* behind him. Without looking up, his father said, "Quit crying like a girl."

The barber, a fat old man with balding hair and a trimmed beard, encouraged him as he cut his hair, "A big boy like you shouldn't bother crying over a haircut. If you don't like it, you have the roots, you know?"

Hasan stared at the mirror and acquainted himself with the emerging boy his father wanted. This boy had a shiny forehead and a stiff upper lip and glared back at him under the fluorescent lights of the barbershop.

When the barber was finished, he said, "You now look like a man."

Hasan saw his father look up and smile in unison with the other men in the shop.

A tall orderly maneuvered the gurney; his biceps flexed as he pushed it. His parents accompanied him on each side, their eyes on him and their hands on its metal railing. His mother touched his arm and asked, "You good, *yavrum?*" She treated him as if he were a little boy, yet still, like most Turkish housewives, she lived for the day her child would get married.

"Yes, *anne,*" he replied, forcing a faint smile.

She squeezed his forearm gently and let go.

"That's my son!" his father said with swagger.

He blinked and smiled, happy he could make his baba proud. His father worked in the shipping department of a curtain factory, packing orders and loading and unloading boxes and equipment; the hard labor showed in his callused hands. Hairy forearms stuck out of his rolled-up sleeves, and his shirt was tucked into washed-out blue denim. Front teeth yellowed by black tea and tobacco peeked out from his off-day five-o'clock shadow.

His father's favorite pastime was watching wildlife documentaries on TRT, the state television channel. The hunting scenes looked especially graphic after color television arrived in the early '80s. One night when he was about ten, Hasan walked into the living room to serve his father tea in a small hourglass-shaped tumbler over a saucer. He pressed his lips together as he concentrated on the glass, paying attention not to spill, until he saw a clan of hyenas devouring a bloody carcass. He tripped on the carpet, and the tea tumbled off the saucer.

His father sprang from the sofa and said, "Watch your step! It's just a TV program." Pressing his handkerchief on the wet spot on the carpet, he sighed and said, "Are you okay?"

Hasan nodded with downcast eyes. He watched the white handkerchief become light brown. His father patted Hasan's back and returned to the television, which now showed a cheetah chasing an antelope. Hasan collected the fallen glass, saucer, and teaspoon and left the room quickly, to ask his mother to serve the tea. His mother, who kissed him on the cheek and told him not to worry that night because she was always the more forgiving one, now walked with his father next to the gurney.

Before he climbed onto the gurney, he had put on a hospital gown as instructed. It wasn't all that different from his public school uniform. They both were dull and intended to make you look like no one in particular, yet they both made him hyper-aware: the black school uniform highlighted his soft green eyes and dirty blond hair, the evidence of his being a Bulgar *muhaciri* or *göçmen*, an immigrant, and the hospital gown made him ashamed, as it was open at the back, except for a couple of loosely tied laces that held it together. He was grateful he was lying on his back and not exposed. His skin was sweaty against the thin sheet of paper over the military green upholstery of the gurney. He slid his hands under the paper and felt the cool, smooth surface.

When he was three, he wanted to be like his sister. He wanted to go to school when she started a few years before him, he wanted to play with paper dolls when she did, and he wanted to wear a skirt when she wore one. His mother, in her deliciously scented red lipstick and brown hair sprayed into a lion's mane, humored him and let him try on a skirt once so that he'd stop his tantrums. He tried to remember if the skirt looked anything like the webbing between his fingers. Was it pink? Was it lined? How short was it? His father yelled at his mother for spoiling him and treating him as if he were a girl.

Lately, his father had wanted to spend more time with him. He took Hasan to the local coffee shop, where men would gather after work. The men smoked, drank tea, and cursed as they played card games and backgammon over thick tablecloths with occasional burn marks from unwatched cigarettes. He hated the smoke, which stank and burned his throat and eyes, and endured probing questions about school and girls. Sometimes he came up with an excuse not to go, like he had homework to do or didn't want to miss his favorite cartoon, *He-Man*. He-Man was the alter ego of Prince Adam, who didn't waste time in a coffee shop; he wore an X-shaped chest harness and fur trunks and used his super-human strength to defend Eternia and Castle Grayskull against his evil nemesis Skeletor. The sneering look on his father's face betrayed his knowledge that his son preferred some stupid cartoon to his company.

Hasan raised his left hand toward the fluorescent light. The pink webbing extended nearly all the way to the middle knuckles of his ring and middle fingers. Both he and his father had similar webbing between their toes, but apparently, people didn't care about your toes when it came to marriage. He thought of ducks' webbed feet and their skillful navigation of the pond near the neighborhood playground, where he used to play when he was seven or eight. He would run his hands through the cool water and watch its movement against his fingers.

The gurney swerved around the corner, causing his hand to wave in the air. He craned his neck backwards. Upside down, the tall orderly said, "Sorry, *arkadaşım*," and grinned. A few wiry chest hairs burst through the V-neck of his scrubs. A set of white teeth flashed through the cotton-candy lips of his mustached and bearded face. Hasan smiled back. As he straightened his neck, he remembered being five and playing with a schoolmate. They were naked on a rug on the floor. They rubbed their bodies against each other. The strands of fabric in hues of pink and beige mingled with one another in the afternoon light. He didn't remember what happened before or after, or where they were exactly. Yet, like the fireflies he would suddenly spot on a summer evening, this memory appeared now and then, making his heart skip a beat and his insides feel warm.

He jolted as the gurney hit the double doors of the operating room with a thud. His parents let go of the gurney. His father waved, and his teary-eyed mother gave him a kiss on the cheek. The orderly said, "See you later, *arkadaşım*," and hurried off. Hasan saw bright lights, movable metal shelves with dozens of knives and tools, and people hidden behind scrubs, masks, and gloves. One of them put her gloved hand on his forehead to make him lie his head down. His heart beat faster, but his body felt languid. He closed his eyes and imagined himself elsewhere, anywhere but here.

He was in front of the kitchen window back home, the wings of which opened onto the fruit orchard at the back of their first-floor apartment. The orchard looked like a fairy-tale forest at night and was shot through with sunrays during the day. It was hot. He was six years old and bored. His sister had homework and wouldn't play with him. Barefoot, he climbed through the window and collected ripe plums that had fallen from the trees. He brought them back to the kitchen, smashed them with his fist, breaking the cloudy purple rinds, and rubbed the soft burgundy flesh against the metal colander, perforated with a flower pattern. He collected the foamy, sweet and sour pulp in the bowl underneath. Again and again, he climbed through the window, down to the garden, and back up to the kitchen, sometimes accidentally stepping and sliding on rotting plums and splattering plum juice all over the kitchen. When his mother returned from the next-door neighbor's, she yelled at his sister for not watching him and at him for making a big mess. She said that only girls made marmalade and that she would tell his father if he ever did something like this again. After sending him to his room, she washed the utensils and wiped the kitchen counter, cabinets, floor, and walls before his father returned from work.

Back in his room, Hasan felt the sting of having angered his mother, who had sounded like his father. He stared at the paper dolls that he and his sister balanced on the windowsill. With names like Maviş, Elif, and Ali, the dolls had unnaturally large eyes that dominated their faces, all with the same posture: arms at their sides, elbows out, and legs slightly open. Their undergarments were already drawn on them. They came with cutouts of paper clothing that he and his sister attached to the dolls' shoulders, arms, and legs by folding paper tabs that stuck out on the edges. Hasan tore them up, one by one, and stamped on the pile of heads, limbs, and outfits. When he got tired, he threw himself on his bed and cried himself to sleep.

Hasan was brought back as the anesthesiologist told him that he would put a mask on his face that looked like the ones pilots wear in the movies. He thought of He-Man flying the Talon Fighter, and nodded. Told to count down from ten, he obeyed as he gazed intently at his webbed fingers:

Ten. A pleasant lightness flooded his mind.

Nine. His fingers became blurry, gradually losing their contours.

Eight. His hand disappeared in the enveloping nothingness, to be forever reformed for adulthood.

BIG SISTER

Tongues started wagging after Nazlı *Abla*, our next-door neighbor's daughter, was hospitalized for a week. I heard her mother tell my mother through the kitchen window that she had a bleeding ulcer. But the real gossip started after her hospital stay. In the year that followed, she broke up with her fiancé, took a job as a secretary, and got a license to drive her father's car.

At twenty-one, Nazlı was eight years older than me and unmarried, so I was to address her as *abla*, big sister. For some people, her name, which meant *reluctant* or *coy*, was the obvious cause of her breakup. The exact interpretation depended on how one saw this young woman who chose a job over marriage, which was unheard of in our neighborhood in Çorlu in 1989 in Turkey. Naturally, her chosen path gave all the women, including my mother and grandmother, a lot to talk about. They expressed surprise and pity and endlessly debated the reasons why she ended her engagement to the "polite young man," as one of them described him. I had met him once at their engagement party, and yes, he was nice enough, but not good-looking enough for her, plus she was taller than him. Anyway, the more I overheard my grandmother and mother have heated discussions with their friends about her, the more invested I became, wondering what exactly had led to her rebellion.

Men weren't supposed to hear these conversations, yet, as far back as I can remember, they took place around me, whenever women gathered at our apartment, usually in the afternoons after I got home from school. When I was younger, I used to nestle between them, indulge in cookies and pastries, and drink black tea diluted with water so that it wouldn't scald my mouth, without registering what they were saying. But, as I got older and started paying attention, I sensed a discomfort in myself, plus the older women seemed to question my presence when they discussed private matters. I was gradually relegated to the next room but still heard through open doors bits and pieces of their conversations, the familiar soundtrack from my childhood. They'd gossip for hours about marital problems, indiscretions, and such, until one of them would eventually sigh and say, "*Çok dedikodu ettik, günaha girdik,*" pointing out the sinfulness of it. Another would insist that it wasn't gossip, just a retelling of what had happened. This exchange would usually signal the end of that session, but the same cycle of admission and denial, confessing and glossing over, would repeat itself day after day, to my amusement.

Çorlu was a small city known for manufacturing and commerce in the northwestern part of Turkey, and most jobs were in retail stores or factories that produced food, cleaning supplies, car parts, and textiles. Our neighborhood was on the edge of town next to vast fields of sunflowers that would be harvested for oil by a nearby factory at the end of the summer. There were four-to-five-floor apartment buildings, a mosque, and a small *bakkal* for groceries. A road, on the side of which Nazlı *Abla* parked her father's Mazda, separated our building from a playground, which had four swings, a seesaw with weathered wooden seats, a rusting slide, and a few tall *ıhlamur* trees surrounding it. I missed the times I spent there as a small child. After school, if the weather was good, I would find my grandmother sitting under a linden tree with her friends as they watched their grandchildren play.

At seventy, my grandmother referred to our neighbors in their fifties and sixties as "children," which always sounded funny. She had piercing hazel eyes that saw through everyone. She was born and lived most of her life in a village in the mountains of the Artvin province in the northeast, away from the modern urban centers of the Republic. Like most women in her village, she was never taught to read and write, and she worked in the grain fields with my grandfather until she came to live with us after his death. Her bent back showed the hard work of her younger years. Whenever she laughed in public or a man who was not a family member passed by, she would cover her mouth with the corner of her headscarf. This was the only time the shy young woman she must have once been peeked through her tough, permanently sun-ravaged, and knowing facial expression. Otherwise, my grandmother ran the show wherever she was, and I loved and feared her for that.

One afternoon after school, I was reading my *Barbar Conan* comic book sitting on the sidewalk with my back against the fence of the playground, on the other side of which my grandmother and two of her friends were relaying to one another the neighborhood news. Nazlı *Abla* walked out of our apartment building across the street in an orange, short-sleeved T-shirt over tight blue jeans, with her red hair clipped into a loose bun that glinted in the noon sun. She threw her oversized purse into the car and drove away in a rush, without greeting the elderly women. This was a big mistake. I looked over my shoulder to see how they would react.

"Look at her. She didn't even deign to say *merhaba* to us. What's more important than taking a moment to greet your elders?" said Necmiye *Teyze* as she adjusted her headscarf printed with a pattern of spring flowers. She wasn't my real aunt, of course, but young people like me were to add *teyze* after the first name of older, married women.

Cemile *Teyze* screwed up her face, as if she couldn't hold back anymore, and said, "Ay, *teyzeler*, is she really an *ablacı*!? What a pity! She's so young and beautiful." The corners of her paisley headscarf secured around her jaw fell open as she shook her head, revealing her jowls above a string necklace weighed down by small gold Republic coins with the head of the founding father Atatürk on one side and "Türkiye Cumhuriyeti 1923" on the other. She was younger than Necmiye *Teyze* and my grandmother, therefore falling into the category of "children."

Ablacı? One who is fond of big sisters? I didn't understand why being an *ablacı* was such a big deal. My curiosity overcame my manners. I stood up and interrupted their conversation, like *Barbar Conan* would take on a menacing horde all by himself. "I like my sisters, at least sometimes. Does that make me an *ablacı*?"

Necmiye *Teyze* sucked her teeth, as if she had seen a ghost, and Cemile *Teyze* laughed loudly, forgetting to cover her mouth.

My grandmother frowned and raised her hand like a judge presiding over a trial, and they quieted down. She said, "No, Gökhan, you are not. You are a man. Men can't be *ablacı*. And don't you ever use that word! Go home and do your homework and stop reading that *fotoroman*."

There was nothing I could do. Having interrupted women's conversation, I couldn't be trusted with the rest of it. I kissed each *teyze*'s hand and touched them to my forehead one by one. As I walked across the street, I looked back and saw that they had resumed their heated discussion. Even if I didn't understand what being an *ablacı* meant, I now had sense enough to know that it would be squashed under the gavel of their judgment over and over that afternoon.

I mulled over the word as I did my homework at the kitchen table. I didn't dare to ask anyone, but remembered my father using another word, *nonoş*, for male celebrities like Zeki Müren and Bülent Ersoy who wore dresses and makeup and acted like women on television. As far as I could tell, a *nonoş* was a man who was less than a man and therefore deserving of ridicule. That is when it struck me that *ablacı* might be an insult the older generations used for women who weren't womanly somehow. I bit into a slice of bread spread with margarine and tomato paste, my favorite after-school snack. I watched my reflection on the old metal tray in the kitchen: my face a blurry, watercolor combination of black bangs over tan forehead, my eyes two dark holes, and my mouth a slit of peach skin smeared here and there with blood-red tomato paste.

The next morning, I pretended I was sick so I could stay home and listen to my mother gossip about Nazlı *Abla*. I felt like I had to get to the bottom of this not only for her but also for myself. Neighbors often came by for coffee after their husbands left for work and their children for school. "Tiny" Ayşe showed up this morning. Her nickname was funny, and she knew it. She was actually as big as, if not bigger than, that fat pop singer who was known for stepping on her little dog.

As I flipped through *Tommiks* in the living room across from the kitchen, I saw her waddle in. She smiled and waved at me. I waved back. My mother had already made coffee. A pair of matching demitasses and their saucers, decorated with a pattern of red tulips, waited on the breakfast table.

"Have you heard it, *abla*?" Just like that, Tiny Ayşe skipped the usual civilities and dove into the gossip. It must be important.

"Heard what?" my mother said as she adjusted the collar of her robe and sipped her coffee from the tiny cup across from the not-so-tiny Ayşe. I couldn't help but smirk.

"Nazlı was seen with an unknown woman downtown the other day." She lowered her voice. "She must be her . . . you know. I can't even say it—Allah help us!"

My mother glanced my way. I was pretty sure she was debating closing the kitchen door. I looked down and pretended to pore over my comic book and prayed she wouldn't shut the door.

"Well, that doesn't necessarily mean she's a *sevici*," my mother said, "Maybe she's just her coworker?"

Sevici. Literally, one who pets.

Tiny Ayşe looked deflated for a moment. She protested, "Ay, *abla*, you always think the best of everyone!" and eagerly continued, "Don't you wonder what they do in bed? I wonder which is the woman and which is the man?"

My mother almost coughed up her coffee. "No, I don't. Neither should you!"

"I wonder if Nezahat *Teyze* knows?" said Tiny Ayşe.

"How would I know? We can't ask her. It's a family matter, and none of our business."

My mother had good sense about such matters. Unlike my grandmother, she knew how to read and write. But when she was twelve, my grandparents made her quit school. In their thinking, girls didn't need to go to high school. She helped around the house and in the fields until she married my father at eighteen. They moved around the country every few years, living in mostly western regions of Turkey, due to my father's job as an army officer. The military had backed the secular democracy since its beginning in 1923, including the third, most recent, coup in 1980. The secular influence of the army in my mother's life made her uncover her hair for good. Every year when school ended and my sisters and I came home waving our report cards, she'd hug us, kiss us on the cheeks, and tell us how she dreamt about becoming a nurse when she was young. She must have wondered how her life would have turned out differently if she had continued school. Instead, she now ministered to the neighborhood gossips.

"She will burn in *cehennem* if she continues with this *sevici* business," said Tiny Ayşe matter-of-factly as she finished her coffee. An aspiring *falcı*, she covered her demitasse with the saucer, flipped them over, and placed them on the table.

My mother said in a hushed tone, "If she is indeed a *sevici*, Allah keep her away from us and our children. Watch your kids around her. We must protect them."

Tiny Ayşe nodded with pursed lips. During the brooding silence that ensued, she fingered the bottom of the overturned demitasse on the saucer a couple of times to check whether the dregs had cooled so that she could read them and practice her fortune-telling skills. I thought about Nazlı *Abla*'s fortune; the image of her burning in *cehennem* made my stomach sick. I went to my room and laid down.

Ablacı. Sevici. Now I was sure about the meaning of the first word because I was familiar with the second. Bullies at my school called girls who were athletic or stood up to them *sevici*. For boys like me who were bad at sports or good friends with girls, the corresponding insult was *top* or *ibne*, a faggot.

I had solved the puzzle of Nazlı *Abla*, but I didn't feel victorious. I wondered if the downtrodden, minor characters in comic books felt a similar dread before their enemies. I was now worried about Nazlı *Abla*—and myself.

I somehow managed to nap that afternoon. And I had a dream. I blamed Tiny Ayşe for it afterward. In my dream, I saw Nazlı *Abla* make love to her girlfriend. She caressed her smooth hair and olive skin, gave her long kisses, and touched her breasts and between her legs. She made her go wild.

I woke up, hot and sweaty, when my mother came into my room to check on me. Realizing I was excited from the dream, I rolled onto my side away from her. She placed a tray of tea and two slices of apple tart on my desk and said that my sisters were back from school. I mumbled that I'd get up soon. I wondered if my sisters knew about Nazlı *Abla* being a *sevici*.

My sisters' room was a shrine to 1980s male pop stars. We all regularly read the Turkish version of the teen magazine *Blue Jeans*, which published pop culture news from abroad. The walls of their room were covered in posters of their favorite male stars—Michael Jackson, Duran Duran, the Pet Shop Boys, Wham! and Don Johnson. *Miami Vice* was their favorite TV show.

I walked in as they were having their tea and apple tart. They both had big curly hair with so much hairspray that I had joked before that their hair would fall off one day and that they'd never need a room deodorant. They were older than me, fifteen and sixteen, and looked and acted like weird twins. They had already changed out of their school uniforms and accessorized; both had hoop earrings and neon pink T-shirts, yellow tights, and baby blue legwarmers. My first thoughts were: I have never seen them exercise; our parents will never let them go out like this; and they looked like fashion disaster twins. I knew better than to tease them, though. I needed them to talk, plus they knew I was pretending to be sick. They snickered when they saw me.

"So, Gökhan, you're feeling better already?" asked Buse, who was the younger of the two.

"We have more important things to talk about," I said.

"Like what?" asked Neşe.

"Nazlı *Abla*," I said.

"Oh, her," Buse said and eyed Neşe as her eyebrows went up.

"What do you mean?" said Neşe.

"Well, people are talking about her, and I heard her called *ablacı* and *sevici*."

"You mean *lezbiyen*," Buse clarified. She turned to Neşe and said, "See, I told you she's strong like a man, like when she used to play volleyball with us."

"What does that mean?"

"She *likes* women, that's what it means," answered Buse, the know-it-all among us.

"*Sus!*" Neşe silenced Buse. Then she turned to me and said, "She's older than us, and mom told us to stay away from her, so you stay away from her, too."

"But I'm not a woman. What's there for me to be afraid of?" I asked.

They both scowled at me in disbelief, and Buse yelled, "Because she's a *sapık!*"

A pervert. I should have known what they would say. Nazlı *Abla*, who was their friend a year ago, was now their enemy. Realizing how quickly everyone had deserted her made my insides simmer.

"I guess," I said as I looked down and scuffed the carpet with my big toe. After a few seconds, I looked up and blurted out, "Maybe you two should never leave this room then, especially looking like the circus clowns you're dressed as at the moment!"

I stormed out and slammed the door, ignoring their protestations.

I left the apartment quickly, ignoring my mother's "What's going on, Gökhan?" I walked around the building to the small community garden at the back, where tenants had planted a few fruit trees, vegetables, and herbs, and was startled to find Nazlı *Abla* smoking there. She was leaning against the building wall in blue jeans shorts and a red spaghetti-strap top. Her bare feet and toes with peeling red nail polish touched the garden soil, with her slippers thrown to the side. She looked sideways at me as she raised her chin and exhaled a thin plume of gray smoke. I used to say hi to her as she smoked there from time to time, and she would ask me about school and such. But this was the first time I had seen her there since her hospitalization.

I walked over hesitantly, as I didn't want to intrude, but I couldn't go back, either, because she had already seen me. I stood a meter or so away from her and leaned with my back and hands against the rough surface of the wall, which was warmed by the afternoon sunshine. The sudden sight of her replaced my anger with nerves, not because of what others said—nothing seemed perverted about her—but because of my embarrassing dream. She continued smoking her almost-finished cigarette. I focused my thoughts on the things I had heard about her, but wasn't sure if I had the courage to ask her about them.

As if she read my thoughts, she asked, "You sure it's okay for you to be seen around me?"

I didn't want to get either of us into trouble, so I said, "I won't tell anyone if you don't." I paused as we eyed one another. When she didn't say anything, I added, "I'm not the person the bullies at school say that I am, either. Are you okay with me being here?"

"People have been avoiding me, so it's a welcome change," she said and rolled her eyes. "Why do they pick on *you*?"

"I'm terrible at sports, but girls like me, so they call me names sometimes."

"They're just jealous."

"I guess," I said. "What about you?"

"What about me?" she said, as if she didn't know what I was talking about.

Was I crossing a line? I didn't say anything and looked away.

"Do you like any of them?" she asked.

"Who?" I pretended not to understand what she was asking.

"The guys in your class. Is there one that you like among them? Who might even like you back? You could perhaps look out for each other."

"I don't know. How do you know you like someone?" I didn't like where the conversation was headed. I felt exposed.

"You just do. It's okay. You don't have to tell me. Just know that sometimes the ones you like or those who say they love you are the cruelest."

"I'm finding out," I said as I marveled at how we thought alike.

We remained quiet for a while. Leaves rustled in the breeze, and sparrows chirped.

Our silence ended when she said, "People will say what they will, but I won't try to harm myself again over what they might think or say. That's for sure." She winked as if her revelation were an inside joke.

"Harm how?" I asked.

"You don't want to know," she said.

I looked into her eyes. Her sadness was overwhelming. I didn't know what to say, so I glanced down and smoothed the soil with my sneaker.

"It's okay. I'm okay now," she said, "Look where it got me. My parents let me be most of the time. I have a job. I'm saving money to buy my own car. And who knows, maybe I'll move out one day. Of course, it's not easy. We still fight about it from time to time. But I can do things that women in our neighborhood can't, or won't."

She took one last drag of her cigarette, rubbed the butt against the wall, and threw it into the vegetable patch. I wished the patch would catch fire and burn down the entire garden, along with all of the words people use to hurt one another.

"See you around, Gökhan, and don't worry too much," she said as she reached over and ruffled my hair.

After she left, I wondered if she meant worrying about her or myself. Replaying our conversation, I realized she meant both of us. Then I thought about the words I had pondered over the past day and a half: *ablacı, nonoş, sevici, top, ibne,* and *lezbiyen.* If a word is repeated often enough, it loses its meaning for a moment, so I whispered each of those words, one by one, over and over as I contemplated a sea of identical weathered brick apartment buildings across from the community garden.

KASTRO

I sat at the back of the bus, and Mert sat next to me. We avoided eye contact. I was wearing his spare underwear and sweatpants and my own soaked T-shirt. The unexpected intimacy of the situation was baffling. We both looked ahead as the bus lurched through the woods toward the highway that would take us and our classmates back to our hometown of Çorlu. Away from the Kastro *mesire yeri*, a picnic area on the northwestern Turkish coast, where, less than an hour ago, I'd tumbled into a stream that flowed into the cold, choppy Black Sea. Caught between the window and him, and all of them, I contemplated my journey, which now, it seemed, was always headed toward this moment.

Because I studied hard and earned top grades, Emel *Hanım,* our homeroom teacher in my ninth-grade class, appointed me *başkan,* the class prefect, for the 1990–91 school year. I enforced the rules when she was absent. I was her ears and eyes during breaks between classes. Being *başkan* meant being neither the teacher nor merely a student. It meant being respected and sought out when I helped others with their homework but also being left out, like when classmates would ditch the last class to go to the movies and didn't want me to report them to the teacher. Every time they addressed me as *başkan,* instead of using Gökhan, my real name, they marked me as different. I both treasured and felt uneasy about my title.

My position shielded me from my classmates' petty fights and cruelty—we were all taught to respect authority—except during the weekly physical education class that I dreaded yet was drawn to. The room where the boys changed into gym clothes was in the basement of the school building. It was unfinished, with bare concrete walls; it didn't have lockers or even a door. I hated changing in the cold with the others around and piling my clothes on the floor amid cobwebs and construction dust. I didn't like my body. It wasn't chiseled like the male bodies my eyes lingered on in magazines, so I didn't want others to see it. They made crude jokes and tussled with one another. I wouldn't engage in this behavior. I was not like them.

Then came the class itself, as if the unpleasantness of the changing room wasn't enough. I was terrible at all sports—*futbol, voleybol, basketbol,* you name it—though not for lack of trying. I didn't want the others to see me fail over and over, class after class. When Oktay *Bey,* the tall, aggressive phys. ed. teacher, yelled, "*Erkek gibi vursana topa!*" Atilla, the burly goalkeeper, laughed at me, and my other classmates joined in. Sure, I could kick the ball harder "to play like a man," but my aim was just piss-poor. Despite this recurring embarrassment—I still wasn't one of the crowd, *and* I was the worst of all—I did enjoy one thing about the class: stealing glances at the outlines of my buff teacher's and handsome classmate Mert's tight sweatpants as they moved. It was exciting and scary. What if they saw me looking and called me an *ibne?* Would they still want me as their *başkan?*

Toward the end of the fall semester, my friend Hasan, a quiet guy with soft green eyes and wispy, dirty blond hair, hung back at the end of phys. ed. He was two years behind me in the seventh grade and nearly as bad at sports as I was, but he didn't seem to care as much. After the others left the locker room, he warned me, "Gökhan, I heard a couple of guys talk about you during recess. I didn't hear what they said, exactly, but your name was being thrown around. They were laughing, too. You'd best watch out."

Hearing my name—Gökhan, the ruler of skies—reminded me how Oktay *Bey* had curled his lips and concluded, to the guffaws of my classmates, "If you continue playing like this, you can forget ruling the land, let alone the skies." That jab had rankled ever since, like a sunburn that wouldn't heal.

I didn't want to be seen alone with Hasan in the changing room, so I said, "I can't talk right now. I've got to go," crammed my gym clothes in my backpack and left him standing there.

We had become friends outside school when he was recovering from a surgery to fix his webbed fingers in the summer of 1989. He sat next to me when I was reading a comic book by the playground. A kid who saw his bandages called him "the *göçmen* from Atlantis" and said that the legendary sunken city must clearly have been located in Bulgaria. Despite the stupidity of that joke, we found the idea of being from Atlantis and having superhuman powers cool. Both fans of pop music, we'd further bonded over Turkish divas who sang about love, longing, and heartbreak: Sezen Aksu, nicknamed "Little Sparrow," whose bangs and ponytail highlighted her pouty rouged lips; Ajda Pekkan, who looked like an ageless beauty queen goddess; and Nilüfer, the gorgeous girl next door with almond eyes. Our tastes in *batı müziği* differed slightly: He was a Madonna fan, and I a George Michael devotee. He had *True Blue*, and I had *Faith*. We exchanged those cassettes at school and talked about songs on the walk home or during weekends in our adjacent neighborhoods. Sitting on a bench by the playground or at the back of his apartment building or mine under trees in communal gardens, we tried with our limited secondary-school English to decipher the lyrics to "Open Your Heart" and "I Want Your Sex," speculating about possible meanings of words, such as *logical*, *natural*, and *dirty*. Some kids at school were calling him *ibne* behind his back. I didn't tell him that, because I didn't want to hurt his feelings, but I did try to avoid being seen with him at school after that. Others avoided him, too. He was probably aware of this rejection but didn't seem to care or show it.

I replayed his warning about our classmates' jeers over and over from the safety of my room at home, considering how to escape becoming another Hasan. A rugged Swiss mountaineer and a sun-kissed Spanish conquistador waved at me from the cover of *Dünya Coğrafyası*, my world geography textbook, which lay among other books scattered on the floor.

I could curse and crack crude jokes, as the others did, but using words like *siktir* bothered me because they were *ayıp* and I was raised not to say shameful things. Smoking in the toilets or at the back of the building was no good, either, because as a *başkan* I was expected to set an example at all times, and getting caught could cause a scandal. Roughhousing simply wouldn't work, because it made me nervous. The most recent fad among my male classmates was to slap each other's crotches with the backs of their hands and run, or to grab one's victim from behind, through the legs, which made him lurch forward. I wouldn't have minded touching or grabbing a few of them down there. What if they saw through me?

That left *futbol* and girls—and, really, those were the hobbies that made men out of boys at my school. As boring as it was, learning about *futbol* was something I could manage. Always the dutiful student, I made it my extracurricular project over the winter. I started reading the *futbol* section of *Fotomaç* diligently, watched dozens of matches on television, and memorized the colors of the sixty-seven major teams. I could identify every player and recite their stats—touches, faults, red and yellow cards, penalties, and goals. My dad was proud because I knew far more than he did, and the fan boys at school were astonished when I proved myself an authority by resolving stupid hallway quarrels about whose team was the best with an avalanche of stats about performance. Even Hasan, who would roll his eyes at the slightest mention of *futbol,* was impressed.

For my fifteenth birthday in February, I received not one but two *futbol* uniforms, one in the navy blue and yellow of Fenerbahçe, from my dad, and the other in Galatasaray's red and yellow, from my uncle. As well intentioned as they were, these gifts were annoying reminders that everyone at school knew I couldn't kick a ball to save my life—nor even to save myself from being jeered at. Being a manly man was a lot of work, but it wasn't all bad. I enjoyed watching the tight, toned bodies of *futbol* players in their wet uniforms, slick with sweat. When they grabbed and hugged each other as they celebrated a goal, my heart would jump. Still, I knew men touching men this way on television was only permissible as an expression of team spirit.

The next step in improving my image was dating. Through mutual female friends I arranged to meet with Canan, a pretty, buxom girl with curly, dirty blond hair, green eyes, and a kind smile. I spent a recess period walking in the schoolyard with her, attracting dozens of inquiring glances. Mert saw me with her and smirked. Did he see through my bullshit? Or was he surprised because she was more his type than mine? The fine gravel that covered the schoolyard crunched under my feet, as Canan and I talked about classes, the weather, and her hobbies—as expected, watching *futbol* wasn't one of them, but she kindly feigned interest when I gabbed about it at the slightest prospect of awkward silence. I concluded that she and Mert would indeed have been the better match, and never met up with her again.

My next date, Aysel, was very interested in me. For a month we went together to events at school and to the local *pastane* for tea and pastries, but something was missing. I didn't feel like putting in more effort. When she asked if we should see a school play together about the heroic efforts of Turkish men and women during the Kurtuluş Savaşı, I said I wasn't interested in the same old rehashed war story about independence fighters. She said she wasn't going then, either. We both ended up going without telling each other, and when she saw me during the intermission with my female friends Leman and Gül, she slanted her head and narrowed her coal-black eyes. I said I was sorry and smiled awkwardly. She left before intermission was over.

If my attempts at dating failed to improve my image because I couldn't commit, my friendships with Leman and Gül helped mitigate the damage, to an extent. They had transferred to my class at the beginning of the year, and we'd bonded over American movies like *Indiana Jones* and *Honey, I Shrunk the Kids.* That they were *erkek Fatma,* tomboys, shifted attention toward them and away from me. I could breathe a little, since nobody could blame me for not wanting to date them—nobody, that is, except the strapping neighborhood butcher, who saw me with them one day and questioned me the next time I was in his shop. When I told him we were all just friends, he said something was wrong with a man who wouldn't take advantage when "*piliçler* were lining up and throwing themselves at you." He leered at me as he continued handling the meat.

On an unseasonably warm day in March, the three of us went to see *The Underachievers,* an American movie about a group of misfits at a night school. We laughed a lot, acknowledging in the darkness of the theater that we too were misfits, of sorts. After the movie, the girls gushed about the dumb blond jock in the film. I stayed quiet, remembering how my body became warm and tingly and my jeans felt tighter as I watched him make out with the cheerleader. This made me think of Mert in his gray cotton sweatpants, which scared me.

I'd learned about *homoseksüellik* and AIDS a few years before, when Rock Hudson died in October 1985. His death made headlines and broke the hearts of many women, including my mother. News reports compared his healthy black-and-white snapshots from the 1950s and 1960s with his more recent, emaciated color photos. During the Friday prayer I attended with my father that week at the Merkez Camisi in downtown Çorlu, the imam made Hudson the subject of his Friday *vaaz*. He warned the gathered men and boys in the *cemaat* against this particular "Amerikan *ahlaksızlığı*." When my eyes wandered toward the men in the mosque, I squeezed them shut, trying to erase the images of backsides and broad shoulders by reciting ever more intently prayers I didn't understand but had memorized in their original Arabic. Now, standing with the girls in front of the theater, thinking of Mert, the blond jock from the movie, Rock Hudson, and the imam's warning about vice, I shuddered at the trio of *homoseksüellik*, AIDS, and death that circled like vultures around my future.

After we parted ways, I headed home, weaving through the busy downtown streets. An older man, perhaps in his thirties, stopped me and asked, "Do you know how to get to Arka Sokak?"

"I'm sorry, I don't know," I said. I had never heard of such a street.

"That's okay." He stepped closer. His hair was slicked back, and he wore tight blue jeans and a shirt open all the way down to his stomach. A pair of mirrored aviator sunglasses hid his eyes and reflected two fisheye images of me—a pair of warped, oversized heads that the surrounding world and my own body seemed ready to squeeze through and explode. My longish black hair clung to my distorted face. My military officer dad was right: I needed a haircut.

"You're so polite and *tatlı*," he said in a slippery tone. He put his right hand on my shoulder and squeezed it, and asked, "Would you like to walk with me to Şehir Parkı?"

"Uhh, *hayır*, I have to go."

I walked away quickly as he stood there simpering. I was nauseated, and the sound of the traffic and people around me felt amplified. This man was what my guy friends called an *ibne* and news reporters called a *homoseksüel*. I hated myself for recognizing him for what he was, revolting as I found him. It took one to know one, right?

Soon after that, Mert asked me to help him with his algebra homework. As my grade's popular athletic kid, he lived up to his name of "manly" or "manful." When he asked for my help, I found it exciting; when it came to math, *I* was the man. I stopped by his apartment before school. We were both *öğlenci*, so we had classes only in the afternoon and could catch up with homework in the morning. His parents weren't home. He was wearing Adidas shorts and a Metallica T-shirt. It seemed as if he had just woken up. The back of his light brown hair was standing up, and his hazel eyes, set deep in his smooth oily skin, lit up when he looked at me. He seated me at the dining table in the *misafir odası*, which was reserved for entertaining guests. Large, cushioned furniture fanned out along the two windowed walls across from the table. A thin lace curtain covered the large bay windows that overlooked the bustling *çarşı* outside, and thick, tasseled curtains were hitched to brass hooks on either side of the window. An imposing vitrine spanned the length of the windowless wall. Shelves on one side displayed a porcelain dining set and a traditional set of *kahve* demitasses behind glass doors. Various keepsakes his parents must have bought during their domestic and international travels stood on the other side—some had English and other non-Turkish words on them. In the middle of the vitrine was a large Sony television, a videocassette player, and a Nintendo console with joysticks and an impressive stack of game cartridges. The marble coffee table in the center of the room dug its mahogany feet into the plush carpet. On a lace runner atop it sat a crystal vase of multicolored papier-mâché flowers.

This was not a typical apartment for my neighborhood. As I had suspected, based on Mert's brand-name clothes and confident demeanor, his parents were well off. He must have gotten whatever he wanted. I eyed the expensive video game console; I had wanted one for a while now but had never asked, because my parents couldn't possibly afford it.

Mert placed his notebook on the table and showed me his attempt to solve the problem set assigned for that day. He stood next to me and leaned on the table. A fair attempt, I thought, as I inhaled his cologne, which made me slightly dizzy. I tried to explain how to solve the equations, but he was restless and asked me to do it. He shuffled around in his shorts while I corrected his homework for him, and joked about the possibility of repaying me by sharing his *Playboy* stash. I laughed and blushed but didn't look up. The man outside the theater flashed in my mind like a celluloid nightmare. I blocked him out. Mert sat on the sectional as I finished his homework, and I caught a glimpse of him adjusting his shorts now and then. Five minutes before we needed to leave, he ran to his bedroom and put on his suit.

We had to wear suits to school, complete with neckties and jackets. As we walked through the *çarşı*, our reflections in the shop windows looked like two boys playing businessmen. The collars of our slightly oversized dress shirts rubbed against our necks, and our Adam's apples bobbed up and down as we drew saliva to spit on the ground. As we walked by the retail shops that flanked both sides of the main road, under the empty gaze of bored shopkeepers, I relished the illusion that I was a buddy of Mert's, an equal. In that moment I believed that I could will away the desire for him that gnawed at me.

Our school trip to Kastro was on a Sunday in April. I'd looked forward to it as a diversion. For most of the one-hour bus ride the sky was gray and rainy, though faint sunlight broke through the clouds now and then. The spring rain had let up by the time we arrived, but it still wasn't a good day for a picnic; the weathered wooden tables were soaked, so we had to eat our sandwiches on the bus.

After lunch, our teachers suggested that we walk around and take a few pictures to make the trip worth the trouble. They told us that *kastro,* an old Greek word, meant *kale,* a castle, and that the name of the park probably referred to the Byzantine fortress in nearby Kıyıköy. I wondered how many men had died over the centuries, defending that fortress and securing the surrounding lands, and whether we'd spot any ruins or tombstones. We didn't. Kastro was a quiet wooded area through which a stream snaked into the Black Sea. Most of my class opted to trek the rocky banks of the stream toward the beach. Our teachers told us to be careful—*dikkatli olun*—and stay in sight—*gözümüzün hizasından çıkmayın*—before they huddled under a tree to smoke. The Black Sea was famous for its eddies and rip currents—not that anyone would go into the water this early in the year, but we all had been warned at the beginning of the trip about the unforgiving nature of the mighty sea and the lives lost on that part of the coast every summer.

In typical fashion, the boys ran ahead and the girls lagged behind, chatting and laughing. I trudged along in the middle. Fortunately—or perhaps unfortunately—my friend Hasan, who'd surely have tagged along beside me, had called in sick and skipped the trip. The stream, swollen with rainwater, flowed vigorously as it approached the sea. Leman and Gül yelled my name. They knew I preferred their company, but like the coward I was, I ignored their calls, and jogged ahead to catch up with the guys. This was when it happened. Atilla, who sometimes sought my help with homework, ran toward me from the side, smiling and waving. I stopped and faced him, thinking that he wanted to talk to me. Instead, he shoved me in the chest with both hands, sending me stumbling over the rocks and into the water rushing by, about a meter below. The freezing water seeped through my jeans, sneakers, and jacket, and knocked the wind out of me. For a few seconds, while I was under, I wondered if this was how death might feel.

Disoriented, I flailed and gasped in the stream's chilling embrace, until someone extended a hand into the water. I grabbed the hand like a lifeline and was yanked up and helped onto the rocks. As I sat, soaked, my fingers wiping silty water from my burning eyes, the view of Mert squatting in front of me, a concerned look on his face, materialized as if through a thin, opaque layer of ice on a windowpane.

Atilla snickered behind him and yelled, "Look, the first person to drown in waist-deep water!" Mert gave him the middle finger. Leman and Gül, who'd seen what happened and run to my side, called him a *hayvan*, an animal, and I yelled, "*Siktir git.*" Everyone seemed taken aback by my rare use of obscenity, despite having just seen what happened and knowing that he no doubt deserved it.

The teachers, who'd seen the commotion in the distance, sauntered up to yell at Atilla, me, and everyone else for horsing around. The gym teacher Oktay *Bey* handed me a towel and told me to clean up. Murat *Bey*, the head teacher, announced that it was time to leave. The weather wasn't getting any better.

As we walked back to the bus, I shivered in the wind.

"You okay, *başkan?*" Mert's eyes met mine briefly.

"Yes," I said quietly, and looked away as another shiver ran through my body.

"Hold on," he said. He rummaged through his backpack. The front zippered pocket sported Metallica, Kiss, and Rolling Stones patches. He pulled out and extended a pair of sweatpants and black boxers, printed with hundreds of tiny red-and-white tongues sticking out of hundreds of mouths. "That's all I have, but here, put them on. I told my mom it was too cold to swim, but she packed these anyway in case I got wet. Maybe her treating me like a child will help this once."

He smiled in a way that begged for a response. I remained silent but accepted his offering. The boxers felt soft and warm in my hands, and the print looked familiar.

Murat *Bey* told the bus driver to let me in to change before the others boarded. In my few minutes alone I took off my T-shirt, wrung it out, and put it back on. I tried putting myself in Mert's shoes—I was in his underwear after all—and wondered at how easily he had offered me something so intimate. Could I ever be so smooth? Could I ever not give a damn what others might think?

As Mert's underwear and sweatpants slowly absorbed the moisture from my wet T-shirt, I thought of Hasan's locker room warning, a few months back. *You'd best watch out.* Realizing that all my efforts had been so transparent, that I had no protective cover whatsoever, was like being shoved into cold water again and again.

When I got home, I went straight to my room and changed quickly. I threw the wet clothes into the laundry hamper. It was good to finally be dry, but I felt as if bedbugs were crawling all over me. I tried not to think about what happened, or about Mert.

When my parents asked about the trip, I said that it'd rained all day, so there was nothing much to tell. We ate dinner as usual in the living room. We didn't have a dining room or a separate room to entertain guests. Our living room overlooked the neighbor's concrete yard and was sparsely decorated. Two brown futons on opposite sides of the room faced each other over wall-to-wall navy blue carpet. In the middle of the room there was a coffee table with a vase of plastic flowers and an ashtray. For meals, we pushed it to the side to make room for the *sofra*, a low, small, circular table we stowed in the pantry; we sat around it on the floor. A clock hung on the light blue wall above one of the futons, and a framed picture of the Kaaba in Mecca, embellished with verses from the Koran in Arabic calligraphy, hung above the other. Otherwise, there was nothing to remind us of the world outside Çorlu except our Grundig television on a stand in the corner. As far as my parents were concerned, other countries and cultures only existed in the televised world.

I tuned in to a movie on Star TV after dinner. My mother, who sometimes did laundry in the evening if she had been too busy socializing during the day, asked about the unfamiliar wet clothes that had been in the hamper. I told her I'd tripped and fallen in the water during the school trip, and a classmate I didn't really know had lent me his spare clothes. She didn't see my pained expression. The thought of what happened turned my stomach into a volcano ready to erupt. She gave me a hug and said that I should've been more careful. I resented being held like a child, so I squirmed out of her embrace.

After she finished the laundry, she sat next to me in the living room, where I was watching *Die Hard*. She told me to return the sweatpants and boxers she had just ironed to the nice boy. She held up the boxers, pinching the elastic band between her index fingers and thumbs, and frowned as if she was trying to solve a puzzle, saying, "Why would anyone wear underwear with so many mouths, or any mouths? It's like the world's upside down!"

Looking away from Bruce Willis for a second, I said, "Yeah, really weird."

As I watched NYPD cop John McClane in a white tank top save his wife and her coworkers from robbers who took them hostage during a Noel party in Los Angeles, I decided to banish any thought of Mert. I resolved not to be friends with him or to repay his kindness by helping him with his homework, or even to return his underwear and sweatpants. He seemed to have multiples of everything—I remembered the huge stack of game cartridges—so he probably wouldn't even miss them. On the way to school in the morning, I threw them into the garbage bin outside our building.

SWEET TOOTH

O ut of the dozens of fellow students Gökhan met during orientation at Boğaziçi University in Istanbul in fall 1993, only Cengiz made an impression. Gökhan was ten minutes early for the final session of the morning and sat close to the exit near the back of the auditorium of the Temel Bilimler arts and sciences building. Students arrived in small chattering groups as he browsed the course schedule, which was printed in English, the language of instruction at Boğaziçi. Gökhan silently debated whether he should pronounce the word *schedule* the mushy British way, which sounded funny, or the crisp American way, which sounded brash. He had heard the word pronounced both ways in his foreign language classes in middle school and high school, but he hadn't needed to choose, until now.

When the auditorium was nearly full, an older woman in a navy blue dress suit walked onstage. At that moment, someone emanating the syrupy scent of Brut cologne dropped into the next seat and sighed, which made Gökhan look. The latecomer brushed a black curl from his forehead.

"*Merhaba, ben* Cengiz."

"*Selam*. Gökhan."

That was all they could manage before the university registrar began her opening remarks. During the parade of short speeches that followed, Gökhan couldn't help but glance from time to time at Cengiz, noticing his fitted orange shirt and the faded Levi's that exposed his right knee. Meanwhile, Cengiz kept shuffling between the schedule and the notebook he scribbled in. After the registrar's office finished its long-winded presentation with a discussion of final exam protocol, Cengiz said, "I've got to make a quick stop at my department. *Görüşürüz.*" He gathered his jacket and backpack and left in a hurry. Cengiz's departure made Gökhan face the prospect of lunching alone. He wondered if they'd meet again.

The Orta Kantin cafeteria was full to the brim, so Gökhan bought two *poğaças*, one with feta and the other with black olives, and a cup of hot black tea and left for the quad, taking small steps to not scald himself. One of the benches that lined the perimeter was miraculously empty, so he ate there and watched the passersby while soaking up the late September sun.

Soon he felt warm and overdressed in his brown turtleneck and blue jeans, and his scalp was itchy under his short black hair. He ran his fingers from back to front, brushing his bangs sideways over his forehead.

When he had finished his *poğaças* and was sipping the last of his tea, Gökhan spotted Cengiz walking his way through the quad and waved. He took in his tall frame and observed his relaxed and confident gait maneuvering through the crowd.

"*Naber?*" said Cengiz as he plopped on the bench. He held a Kit Kat bar in his hand.

If Gökhan hadn't seen him, the Brut would've given away his presence.

"*Iyiyim*, a bit tired. You?"

"Same," said Cengiz as his eyes panned over the quad. "So, what do you think of this place?" He sounded skeptical, like an indecisive customer sizing up merchandise.

"It's pretty. People seem nice."

"Well, isn't most everyone, at first?" Cengiz's face wore a playfully charming expression. He unwrapped the Kit Kat and bit into it with gusto.

"True," said Gökhan but couldn't think of anything else to say.

"I'll major in biology. What's your major?" asked Cengiz.

"English literature."

"So . . . novels and stuff?"

"Yeah."

"What will you do with that later?"

Not this question again. People in Çorlu, his hometown, who neither read nor wrote beyond daily exigencies, frequently posed it to Gökhan.

"Teacher? Translator? I haven't decided, yet. What will *you* do with bio?" said Gökhan and raised an eyebrow.

"Umm, scientist, I suppose," said Cengiz, mock-creasing his forehead as if this was the first time he had ever considered the possibility. He leaned back, took another bite of his Kit Kat, and continued, "Why literature?"

"I don't know, I like reading," said Gökhan. "What about you?"

"I like learning how organisms work," said Cengiz in earnest with a sweeping, almost theatrical gesture of his hand toward the quad, "you know, what makes all these creatures, including us humans, tick."

The lawn was full of students, some lounging in the shade of the evergreens and others sheltering their faces or necks from the sun with their notebooks. A stray cat looking for food brushed against legs and feet, and a dog slept under a soon-to-turn deciduous tree.

"Interesting," said Gökhan. "I was in the literature division in high school but still had to take bio. I'll probably take it again to fulfill my science requirement here."

"What do you remember most?"

"DNA, cells, stuff that everyone should know."

"Nice. Exactly what I'm interested in. The stuff we can't control. Like our genetic makeup and instincts."

"Cool," said Gökhan and checked his watch. The afternoon session was about to start. He suggested walking back together. Cengiz deftly threw the last bite of the chocolate bar into his mouth, and they took one of the crisscrossing paths of the quad toward Temel Bilimler. Other first-year students, with the course schedule tucked under their arms, strolled to their respective schools' orientations in different parts of the campus.

Gökhan didn't expect the campus to be so old and beautiful. His high score on the annual national college exam qualified him for the Western Languages and Literatures Department at Boğaziçi. It was the top English program in the country, so he hadn't even bothered to take the three-hour bus trip from Çorlu to visit campus prior to orientation. Now a state university, Boğaziçi was formerly Robert College, which was founded in the nineteenth century as the first American secondary school outside the United States. It was on the European side of Istanbul, perched on the wooded hills that flanked the Bosphorus

Strait. The panoramic view of the waterway down the hill featured a couple of suspension bridges, two old Ottoman citadels, and seaside *yali* mansions with ornate woodwork, as well as newer villas with private pools and manicured lawns in gated communities. The section of campus with tree-canopied benches facing the strait, where students often read or socialized outside class, was called the *manzara*. Some residence halls had views of the Bosphorus, too, which made Gökhan think of old Turkish movies with rich male protagonists who dazzled poor and innocent ingénues who had just migrated from small towns or villages in Asia Minor.

The reality of dorm life turned out to be less glamorous, however, as students were not allowed to choose their first-semester housing. Together with Cengiz, he was placed in the unimaginatively titled Dördüncü Yurt, or "Fourth Dorm," a sprawling two-story building that was built into a steep hillside. The larger upper floor consisted of a single high-ceilinged room that was previously a gymnasium, along with a restroom on the side of the building that faced the Bosphorus. The smaller lower floor had the showers and storage. Indeed, the upper floor looked just like the stomping grounds for jocks and their cheerleader girlfriends in American movies from the '80s, except for the dozens of bunk beds and lockers.

On their first day in the men's residence hall, they discovered, to their amusement, that the corner restroom had the only clear view of the Bosphorus in the building.

"If only the urinals faced the other way," said Cengiz to Gökhan as they relieved themselves, with the windows to their right and behind. They had to strain their necks sideways to see Rumeli Hisarı, an Ottoman maritime fortress, on the hillside and, behind it, the Fatih Sultan Mehmet suspension bridge—named after the twenty-one-year-old Ottoman ruler who conquered the city in 1453.

"Enjoy it while it lasts!" said Gökhan. "This is probably the only time in our lives we'll be able to afford to live in a place like this with such magnificent views."

"I do hope I won't ever live in a restroom," said Cengiz.

Gökhan laughed and stuck his tongue out at him over the shoulder-high partition between them as he zipped his pants.

The gigantic towers and taut steel cables of the Conqueror Bridge, as it was called for short, glinted in the distance as it straddled the strait from Europe to Asia Minor.

Gökhan thought of their residence hall as a bizarre social experiment in which sixty young men from across Turkey were brought together in their first year away from home to somehow learn to live in a single oversize room for an entire semester. Initially, he was shy about dressing and undressing since there were no walls, nowhere to hide, but this open communal living also brought back memories of his high-school locker room, of Mert and Hasan—he wondered where they were now. He didn't let himself follow that thought further. Being a military brat, he knew who he was supposed to be: a man's man who flaunted his interest in drinking, soccer, and women. Like his father, an officer in the army, who yelled at the TV when Beşiktaş, his favorite team, lost and toasted when they won, and slapped him on the back while pointing at the models on the screen during commercial breaks.

When Gökhan reached puberty, his father talked to him about sex in clipped, portentous sentences. "If you don't pull out, the woman will get pregnant," he said.

Gökhan, who was twelve at the time, nodded and averted his eyes.

His father moved on to the subject of cleanliness, touching the tip of his index finger with his thumb and saying, "Make sure to shave your pubic hair regularly. If they are longer than a grain of barley, it's *günah*."

Sin? While his father drank and didn't pray, except during Ramadan, he made sure to give his only son clear instructions regarding the ablutions required after any sexual activity, including masturbation or a wet dream.

"Wash your body thoroughly, rinse inside your mouth and nose three times, and ask Allah to cleanse you."

His father ended the talk with a final note, "Don't forget: Our religion doesn't approve of *livata*."

Gökhan didn't know the word but remained silent. He looked it up in the dictionary afterward and wondered what prompted his father to mention sodomy.

Following the incident during the school trip to Kastro, where a bully had pushed him into a stream, he dated a few girls in high school.

Kissing and fondling in the park or at house parties were exciting transgressions, but the slippery wetness of spit was unpleasant. To preserve her virginity for marriage, no girl in her right mind would go all the way, which he was fine with, so he didn't explore further. Even if it was all everyone talked about in high school, dating felt inessential.

As Gökhan adjusted to dorm life, the near-complete lack of privacy led to some interesting knowledge about others: who had the biggest balls, literally (the general consensus was that it was Mithat, in whose absence tongues wagged about the possible medical causes); who snuck out to drink and get high; who had a hot temper; who had girlfriend problems; who was or passed himself off as a womanizer; and who kept to himself. In this environment, Gökhan inevitably saw Cengiz naked many times. On one occasion, he stared a bit too long at Cengiz, who noticed and responded with a smile. Gökhan quickly turned away.

Gökhan spent most of his first semester enjoying Cengiz's company outside classes and during weekends. They went to movies and art exhibits and frequented cafés in Taksim. Cengiz loved chocolate bars and desserts and insisted on sharing, and Gökhan couldn't refuse—a bite was just a bite. Reiko, an exchange student from Japan in Gökhan's Survey of English Literature class, begged to differ; she called Cengiz and his predilection for sweets "funny." After seeing Cengiz offer him cake in the cafeteria many times, she warned Gökhan, "Your funny friend eats sweets all the time. If you don't watch, you'll both get fat soon."

Cengiz was a fan of the soundtracks to Andrew Lloyd Weber's musicals. He made Gökhan a mixtape of *The Phantom of the Opera* and *Cats* from the tapes a friend's older sister who studied journalism in London had sent. Gökhan found the idea of an entire musical about cats at best whimsical and at worst stupid, but *The Phantom* intrigued him.

"What's it about?" he asked and bit into a Twix bar Cengiz handed him.

Despite what Reiko said, a Twix had two bars and so was perfect for sharing. They were at Orta Kantin for a snack following an afternoon class. A tabby cat napped on their table, and a few students were studying or chatting at other tables.

"Hmm, how do I summarize it?" Cengiz twirled the bar like a baton. "It is about a brilliant musician with a terrifyingly deformed face. He haunts the Paris Opera House. He loves Christine, his beautiful ward and an inexperienced opera singer. But alas, she's in love with Raoul, a young, handsome aristocrat." He bit the tip of his Twix.

"Sounds tragic."

"*Evet*, but the music is beautiful."

"How does it end?"

"The phantom demands that Christine stay with him. He threatens to kill Raoul. What does Christine do? She kisses him!"

"He must've looked handsome and mysterious with that mask on," said Gökhan.

Cengiz gave him a sideways look and raised his bushy eyebrows.

"What?" said Gökhan and took another bite.

"Nothing." Cengiz put his hands through his hair, gathering it into what was almost a proper ponytail before letting it loose again, and said, "Anyway, this is the phantom's first experience of kindness and compassion, so he sets them free and disappears."

"Cool. So, it's about love."

"*Evet*. The unrequited kind. And learning what love really is. And, umm, how you can't make someone like you," said Cengiz. He eyed Gökhan from time to time as he quietly ate the rest of his Twix.

Feeling Cengiz's gaze, Gökhan smiled and gave a quick thumbs up. A guy and a girl who sat at a table across the room packed up their textbooks and left for another class. Cengiz and Gökhan followed suit.

In the spring semester, Gökhan roomed with Cengiz alone in another residence hall. A sofa and a bunkbed dominated their new, small room, a welcome change from the gymnasium setup. Gökhan slept on the upper bunk, and Cengiz below. Cengiz's hair got longer that semester; shiny, black curls cascaded around his face. He also started plucking his eyebrows.

On a Sunday afternoon, Gökhan met with Cengiz, who had just returned from visiting his parents in the seaside Moda neighborhood on the Anatolian side of Istanbul. They sat at the second-floor café in Mephisto Kitabevi, a bookstore in Beyoğlu, Taksim. Their table overlooked the crowds milling about on Istiklal Street, the main drag for shopping and entertainment. As they people-watched, Cengiz said, "Yesterday, we were having breakfast in the kitchen in front of the television, and my mother asked me if I was plucking my eyebrows. I almost choked on my toast."

"What? How did you respond? I mean, other than saying yes."

Cengiz dug into a slice of chocolate cake with his fork and said, "Here, have some."

Gökhan took the fork and complied.

"What could I say? You don't need a guide to a village you see in the distance, as the saying goes," said Cengiz.

"Imagine that, a whole village with beautifully plucked eyebrows," said Gökhan.

"I actually pretended I didn't hear and tried to change the subject. She wouldn't let it go. She said she'd take me to a therapist if necessary."

"*Allah'ım.*"

"Not happening, but I said I'd let her know to get her off my back. Fortunately, *Valentina*, her favorite show, came on, so she moved on."

"All hail badly dubbed Mexican telenovelas."

Cengiz rolled his eyes and said, "Let's share the last bite."

Gökhan had met Cengiz's mother. She was an elementary school teacher with watchful eyes behind horn-rimmed glasses. She had visited a few times since the beginning of the academic year and called the dorm frequently. Each residence hall had a single phone line that could only receive calls. When it rang, the hall security attendant would page the resident's name. If Cengiz was out, which happened often, his mother would ask for Gökhan. She wanted to know where her only son, *gözünün nuru*, the light of her eye, her Genghis Khan, went at all times, whom he went with, and when he returned. During one such call, she complained to Gökhan that she had offered to buy Cengiz a cell phone, which was just becoming available and would thus constitute a major expense, so that they could communicate easily, but Cengiz had told her he would shut it off and not use it. After he hung up the communal phone in the foyer, Gökhan shuffled in his slippers back to their room and thought about this audacious response to parental authority. He wondered if he'd have had the nerve to do the same if he were in Cengiz's shoes.

Strangers also noticed Cengiz. At times when they were off campus, especially on the conservative outskirts of Istanbul, people stared at him disapprovingly as he threw back his hair or licked pink cotton candy off his fingers. When this happened, Gökhan remembered watching stories on the evening news as he was growing up about the death of *travesti* sex workers that portrayed their grief-stricken, protesting friends as freaks who were likely doomed to a similar fate at the hands of their *müşteri* tricks or the police. The onlookers interviewed by reporters would call them *ahlaksız*—immoral—or *sapıklar*—perverts—and scream for the government to cleanse the city of their dirty presence. During the local elections in March, the pro-Islamic Refah Partisi, the Welfare Party, won the mayorship of dozens of cities, including Istanbul, and a sizable percentage of the nationwide vote, so the rising influence of religious conservatism was palpable. Gökhan worried that somebody would curse at Cengiz or, worse, do him physical harm. He wished Cengiz would curtail his flamboyant manner for his own protection.

For all but the most stubbornly blind observers, the direction of Cengiz's affections was readily apparent, particularly when it came to his frequent seismic crushes on men. He first fell for a neuroscience graduate student he worked with in the biology lab on campus, and Gökhan heard him make comments in passing.

"The new TA I work with is so brilliant, and I want to get to know him more, but he won't socialize outside the lab."

Gökhan could imagine the scene in the lab: Cengiz would euthanize mice in preparation for the day's work and would inevitably make sheep's eyes at the graduate student as they spent the day slicing up diminutive brains together. Gökhan found this idea highly amusing, but when they came across the graduate student together on campus one day, he gained a more well-rounded perspective on Cengiz's interest: the graduate student was good-looking and seemed nice, too—perhaps too nice to say anything about Cengiz's not-so-subtle advances. Cengiz was shaking visibly during their brief chat, and Gökhan felt bad for him. Nothing came of Cengiz's crush on the graduate student. Unfazed, he moved from one infatuation to another, talking to Gökhan endlessly about the man of the moment.

Meanwhile, Gökhan made attempts at dating college women, convinced that he was going to meet the right one soon. Classes and student organizations, like the Art Club or the Ballroom Dance Club, offered plenty of opportunities to meet bright and beautiful women. Early in the spring, he asked out Ilkay, a classmate in Modern Drama. True to her name, which meant "first moon," she was pale-skinned, and she had green eyes and shiny straight hair like the models who would whip around their coiffed manes in shampoo commercials. Gökhan found her name romantic, and she was beautiful, so he thought it could work.

When Cengiz heard about Gökhan's plans with Ilkay, he wanted to join them, but Gökhan told him it was a date, which elicited a quizzical look from Cengiz. During the date, they talked about classes they liked and complained about homework and disorganized professors. It could've been a meal out with any classmate. He was polite toward Ilkay, and she was gracious, but as the dinner went on, he felt like he was leading her on. After the date, their interactions were limited to awkward pleasantries when they saw one another in class.

Later in the semester, Cengiz's newest crush was a fellow biology major. After hearing Cengiz gush about his new acquaintance for a few weeks, Gökhan finally got the chance to see what the big deal was about. They were sitting on the "steps," the amphitheater-style seats in front of the Temel Bilimler building that overlooked the quad, when Cengiz grabbed Gökhan's arm and pointed enthusiastically into the crowd. Serdar looked like a Benetton model with spiky hair, nerdy thick-rimmed glasses, a bomber jacket, and cargo pants. Serdar waved at Cengiz and walked by; Gökhan wondered whether such a well-dressed man would be into guys or girls. He learned the answer a few days later, when Cengiz invited Serdar to hang out in their room, and he showed up with Yeşim, his beautiful girlfriend.

While alcohol wasn't allowed on the premises, Serdar and Yeşim snuck a few bottles of Efes beer, a bottle of vodka, and some orange juice in their backpacks. Gökhan and Cengiz had some peanuts and sunflower seeds to go with the drinks. Gökhan didn't know them at all, so he felt awkward and sat on the lower bunk, drinking most of the beer. The others indulged in the hard liquor as they sat around the old wooden desk by the window and gossiped about the biology department.

Around midnight, after a couple of rounds, Yeşim switched to Serdar's lap, and Cengiz, who wasn't a heavy drinker, said he was dizzy and stretched out on the sofa. After a few more rounds, Cengiz passed out and Gökhan clambered to his bed, at which point Serdar and Yeşim stumbled into Cengiz's bunk and started making out. Gökhan tried to fall asleep, but hearing Serdar be intimate with Yeşim in the bed below him, he felt nervous and warm and needed air. He got up and left the room.

Around 3:00 a.m., Gökhan was chatting in the study room with a mutual friend, a philosophy major who had a habit of studying late after clubbing, and Cengiz walked in looking groggy and uncharacteristically disheveled.

"I'm sorry," said Cengiz on the way back to their room. "They're gone. I didn't think they'd start having sex. They woke me up and told me you had left."

"It's okay," said Gökhan. "I thought I shouldn't be there, and I couldn't really tell them to stop, either, so I decided to remove myself until they were finished. Are you okay?"

Cengiz looked down and sighed. He seemed defeated. Gökhan patted him on the back as they walked back into their room. As soon as Gökhan closed the door, Cengiz turned around and pulled him in, hugging him in the semi-darkness. They lingered for a few seconds until Gökhan felt Cengiz's lips on his lips, his stubble on his skin, and his arms around his neck. Cengiz was a little taller than he was. Gökhan's breathing got heavier when Cengiz started caressing his back and pulled off his T-shirt. Gökhan didn't protest and slid his jeans off. Not knowing what to do next, he sat on the sofa and watched Cengiz undress. The boundaries of friendly affection, already blurred, faded in the moment when both were naked, and a pleasurable urgency Gökhan had never felt with anyone else before soon overrode everything.

At dawn, Gökhan woke up in his bunk to the sound of the call for morning prayer that seemed to travel and swirl in the wind. Taking care not to wake Cengiz, he got up, showered, and did his ablutions. It felt good to be clean. There were still two hours before his morning class, so he returned to the warmth of his bed and pondered the previous night's events. Outside their window, *erguvan ağaçları*, Judas trees, in full purple bloom swayed in the wind in the *manzara* while the mighty Bosphorus down the hill streamed quietly against the rising sun.

Mixed feelings collided and threatened to pull him apart. He had enjoyed intimacy with another man and wanted more, but he felt a profound guilt at the thought of his parents, especially his father. What about Cengiz? How would this change their friendship? And what would others think about them or say to them if they found out? After an uneasy hour compounded by the worry that Cengiz could wake up at any moment, he resolved to skip his Friday classes and leave town for the weekend. He changed quickly and tossed a few clothes and a textbook in his backpack. He couldn't go to his parents' house—he didn't want to deal with their probing questions and exhortations to overeat, much less his already worsening feelings of shame, so he opted to visit his uncle's family on the Anatolian side of Istanbul. He went there every couple of months, and he'd be back by Sunday, so he decided he didn't need to tell Cengiz where he was going.

His uncle, aunt, and two adult cousins lived in the middle-class İçerenköy neighborhood, a former village that long ago had been swallowed by Istanbul's sprawl. His uncle, a high school principal, and his aunt, a retired textile worker, asked him about school and his plans after college graduation. School was going well, and graduation was far away, thankfully. They otherwise let him be. His cousins took him out to eat and shop at an *alışveriş merkezi*. The recently built shopping mall was located in a new housing development with high-rise apartment buildings. Such luxury *rezidans* projects swarmed the empty areas around the E5 and TEM highways that connected the old, coastal Istanbul to its suburbs.

Gökhan's cousin Mustafa, a twenty-five-year-old accountant with thick-rimmed glasses and a receding hairline that revealed a shiny forehead, was engaged to be married soon. His fiancée, Pınar, a bank teller, met Mustafa in the mall, dressed in a pantsuit and heels. They joined Gökhan and his other cousin, Semra, for a quick but pricy Burger King meal before they left to do some wedding shopping. Semra, in her first year at Marmara University and majoring in education, was an avid shopper who never missed an opportunity to look at high-heeled shoes and handbags. Her cobalt-blue contact lenses, heavy makeup, and dyed blond hair attracted attention wherever she went, but underneath it all, she was whip-smart, concentrating on math education in her studies. Gökhan was happy to go along as she hunted for the next shoe-handbag combo. They strolled through the mall's shiny perfumed halls, where Muzak constantly played.

When they tired of walking, they stopped by the Mudo patisserie in the food court and grabbed coffee. Semra got a skinny latte and paid for Gökhan's espresso.

When Gökhan protested, she said, "You're visiting. And let me pay for a change. Eşref never let me pay."

"Okay, but why the past tense?" said Gökhan.

"Let's sit first," she said. After they found a cozy spot by the back corner, Semra said, "We broke up."

"Sorry to hear. What happened?"

"You were right."

"What?"

"Remember when Eşref and I first started dating, you said he had such an old-fashioned name? That he reminded you of TV shows with *maço* men who ruled over their women?"

"Yes. And?"

"Well, he did turn out to be a bit like that. He got jealous because men approach me all the time. Not my fault."

"Of course not."

"I also do better than him in everything at school. Again, not my fault."

"You're the whole package, and he should appreciate that," said Gökhan.

"It's not like I didn't try," said Semra, "but whenever I tried to talk to him about it, he'd shut down. I finally realized his ego wasn't going to let go."

"I'm sorry it didn't work out."

Semra contemplated her latte for a minute before she said, "Eşref is not the first guy to be that way, and he won't be the last. It's just I liked him very much, more than I did others before, but he just refused to see me for who I am, beyond his idea of me based on all this, you know?" She raised and waved her open hands in front of her face and chest, which made Gökhan laugh. She said, "I'm getting over him. What about you?"

"Not much, really," said Gökhan. "I'm focusing on my studies."

"Okay, based on that evasive response, I see that there is someone new in your life," said Semra, "but I'll let you tell me about her when you're ready."

"Deal," said Gökhan and finished his espresso.

Semra clapped and said, "So I'm right? How exciting!" She squinted at Gökhan and said, "Like I said, whenever you're ready." She picked up her to-go cup and suggested that they continue strolling through the mall.

Semra hung on Gökhan's arm like they were a couple. His cousin was like a sister to him, but not knowing better, female shoppers would smile at them approvingly, while men ogled her and cast jealous glances his way. The strangers' misperceptions amused him, until he caught himself regarding some of the men in a way he had never allowed himself to before. When one or two seemed to return his gaze, his blood blazed because of his altered sense of possibilities, however uncertain. How easy and difficult it is to be one thing on the inside and another on the outside, he thought.

Over the course of the weekend, he realized this unnamed state was his new normal. He felt freshly grounded and exhilarated, like visiting a place for the first time yet feeling at home, but he knew he couldn't confide in his cousins or anyone else, which made him feel unmoored. Late Sunday night, he took the municipal bus back to campus. The midway point of the two-hour trip was crossing the Boğaziçi Bridge, which soared from Asia to Europe high above the dark waters of the Bosphorus Strait, flanked on either side by neon city lights. As the bus sped as if through the air, he contemplated what he had been drifting toward all along: a fundamental secret that, if revealed, would have serious ramifications, with Cengiz at its center.

When Gökhan arrived back at the residence hall, it was past midnight, and Cengiz was asleep. He closed the door quietly and went straight to bed. When he woke up in the morning, Cengiz had already left for class. For the next couple of days, Gökhan stayed out late studying in the library and slipped into the room late at night, with Cengiz always seeming to be deep asleep. He knew they should speak about what happened at some point, but, not knowing how to have that conversation, he was grateful for this elaborate dance of mutual avoidance.

On Wednesday, Gökhan had just finished his lunch and was sipping hot black tea at the *manzara* when Cengiz sat down next to him on one of the benches facing the Bosphorus. Gökhan was pleased to see a generous slice of tiramisu in the transparent plastic container Cengiz laid on the seat between them.

"I want to tell you a story," said Cengiz. "Will you listen?"

"Of course," said Gökhan.

"I had this best friend in high school. I liked him, and I think he liked me, too. But once we both knew it, it became a burden. He stopped coming over to study, ignored me at school, and began dating a girl. I know he was scared. So was I. But I was so hurt that he dropped me as a friend. I still am."

"I'm sorry to hear that," said Gökhan. He thought of his friend Mert and his best friend, Hasan, from high school again, this time with guilt. He distanced himself from them after the incident at Kastro, and Hasan disappeared that summer.

"It's okay. I was young and stupid. What did I expect? That we would be together and live happily ever after? Anyway, I'm telling you this because I need to ask you: Will you promise me you won't stop being my friend?"

Gökhan looked away for a moment and then looked back and said, "I don't know where I'll end up, but I'd never do that to you." He looked away again. "I like you, and I want to be your friend. I know that."

"That's all I wanted to hear," said Cengiz as he opened the container and passed a plastic spoon to Gökhan.

"You know, Reiko's still surprised that I eat so much dessert!" said Cengiz.

Gökhan observed that lately, Cengiz and Reiko had been bonding over Turkish coffee during study breaks in the garden outside the library. Cengiz would tease her by calling her his Japanese aunt because she'd always say he put too much sugar in his coffee. Relieved about the change of topic, Gökhan said, "Well, I was surprised, too, when I first met you. But at this point why is she still talking about it?"

"Apparently, in Japan, boys are supposed to abstain from sweets as they grow up and become men."

Gökhan paused for a moment. The trees in the *manzara* were in full bloom. Down the hill, sunshine reflected off the water that streamed quietly, and freight ships and oil tankers slowly wound through the strait. New construction dotted the hills beyond the water. He slowly raised the spoon in his right hand, let it hang in the air, and said, "Does Reiko know all Japanese men?"

"She's not that kind of a woman, you know?" said Cengiz.

"I mean, how can anyone be sure that *all* Japanese men do that?" said Gökhan.

"If they do, that'd be a life lived bland," said Cengiz.

"I agree," said Gökhan.

They looked at each other and chuckled. They spooned the last bites of tiramisu, chewing the wet, spongy ladyfingers, and savored the bittersweet taste of coffee, alcohol, and sugar.

VULCAN

Ateş put his arm around his girlfriend, Meral. They sat across from me behind a steaming kettle on the coffee table. Five mugs and a wicker bowl of assorted teas stood next to the kettle.

It was the late spring of 1999, and we were at my friend Ali's apartment in the Beşiktaş neighborhood of Istanbul. A few abstract paintings by Ali's girlfriend, Arzu, hung on the wall; colorful, kinetic geometric shapes floated against the yellow walls of the living room. I was the fifth wheel, the bachelor of this group of twentysomethings.

Arzu tipped boiling water into the mugs. I grabbed a bag of Lipton black tea and steeped it in a chipped mug.

Arzu looked at Ateş and Meral and said, "Get a room, you two."

Ali said, "Some like it hot."

I followed, "Meral, you should know not to play with fire." Ateş's name meant "fire."

Meral smiled while Ateş, whose lips glistened with ChapStick, made a sizzling sound as he pointed his index finger at me.

Ateş and I sat inside while the others smoked on the balcony. He looked at me and said, "You should grow a beard, Gökhan. It'd look good on you."

"*Teşekkürler,* I tried once, but the itching drove me crazy." I hadn't known him long, so his comment was unexpected.

"Push through it next time. I'd like to see it," he said.

"*Tamam,* I'll give it a try," I said. "Actually, you're not the first guy to suggest that."

"Who else?" he said.

"You wouldn't know him." It was Cengiz, my friend and roommate from Boğaziçi University. Cengiz was now in America for his doctoral studies in neuroscience; he was tired of his mother pestering him to assuage her fear and guilt that she had raised an *eşcinsel,* a *homoseksüel.* He also wanted to postpone his compulsory military service, so he left as soon as we graduated. I missed him.

"Is it Tolga?" asked Ateş.

"*Negatif,*" I said. "How do you know him?"

Tolga was in the arts education program and moonlighted as a catalog model for men's clothing brands like Sarar and Damat. Ali, Arzu, and I were studying art at Mimar Sinan Güzel Sanatlar Üniversitesi, a public fine arts university named after the famed Ottoman architect and engineer, on the shore of the Bosphorus in Beşiktaş.

After Cengiz left, I applied and got into Mimar Sinan for my master's in art history. My parents wanted me to become an English teacher, but I said I'd do something in tourism, so art history after English would be relevant; they seemed satisfied with that.

Ateş and Meral studied architecture at Yıldız Technical University, up the hill from Mimar Sinan. Out-of-town college students either lived in a residence hall, like Arzu, or rented off-campus, like Ali and me. If they were from Istanbul, like Ateş and Meral, they commuted from home.

"I visited Ali and Arzu on campus," said Ateş. "I recognized Tolga from the magazine ads when they introduced us."

"Good eye," I said.

He laughed and said, "He's so tall. He's hard to miss."

Ateş was without Meral the next time we met at Ali's, a couple of weeks later. We gathered in the evening and drank beer and ate sunflower seeds until our tongues felt rubbery.

Ali had applied to American MBA programs in arts management and was eagerly awaiting news. He and Arzu were planning to marry this summer after graduation.

Ateş said, "I may go to England to study architecture."

"What about Meral?" I said.

"She's great, but it didn't work out," he said.

"What happened? Was she not *tiki* enough for you?" teased Ali.

Tiki was how we humorously referred to students who came from rich families. The ones who drove to campus instead of taking public transportation, maintained tans year-round, sported expensive name brands like Adidas and Benetton, and went on ski trips to Uludağ in winter. I wondered just how *tiki* Ateş was.

"That's not the problem, she's way more *tiki* than I am," said Ateş.

"Is it because you're thinking about going to Ingiltere?" asked Arzu.

"She could go with you," said Ali.

"Yes, except I didn't ask her," said Ateş. "And she broke up with me, saying something was missing, that we'd be better off as friends." He avoided eye contact.

Later, he cornered me in the kitchen as I was rummaging through my friend's cupboards for napkins.

"How's Mimar Sinan?"

"It's good," I said.

"And Tolga?" he asked.

"He's fine, he said hi," I said as I looked him in the eye and walked around him back to the living room.

Around midnight, Ali and Arzu told us we could crash in the living room and retreated to his bedroom. Ateş and I sat across from each other at the coffee table with our thumbs, index fingers, and lips blackened from plying sunflower seeds for the past two hours. He stared at me with an amused, drunken grin. I smiled and said I'd be right back, leaving for the bathroom to wash up.

I found him waiting at the bathroom door after I was finished. He pushed me back in gently. He closed the door and drew close to me. He was shorter than me, with wide, solid shoulders. He leaned forward on his toes and kissed me. The wetness of his warm, slippery lips rubbed against my two-week beard. I felt the heat spread from his mouth to my body.

He pulled away abruptly, put his index finger to his lips, and kneeled in front of me. As he unbuckled my pants, the tightness of my jeans and briefs gave way to gooseflesh, and an electric charge ran through my body. He grabbed my hips with his hands and started sucking me. I balanced myself with my right hand on the cool porcelain sink, and my left hand caressed his close-cropped hair as his head moved back and forth.

I closed my eyes under the bathroom lights that glowed like the sun. As the orange heat intensified behind my eyelids, I couldn't hold on any longer and released.

He swallowed, got up, and kissed me. "Buckle up," he said and left the bathroom.

I cleaned up quickly and followed him to the living room. I had volunteered to sleep on the recliner by the window, but Ateş pulled out the sofa bed, put two cushions against one of the armrests as makeshift pillows, and spread the sheet Ali had left. I hesitated. *Did we dare, with our friends in the other room?* It didn't take much to suppress that thought when Ateş laid on his back on one side of the sofa bed and patted the other side.

I laid beside him, leaned over, and kissed him. "This explains why Meral broke up with you."

"I tried my best, but she's not stupid, she knew," said Ateş.

"Am I your first?" I asked.

"Yes. You?"

"Wow, you know your way."

"Well, it's not rocket science. We both have the same equipment."

"I've never thought about it that way. You should write a book."

"Maybe I will," he said.

"And to answer your question, I've been with men before, but nothing serious." I didn't want to go into what I had with Cengiz because we had avoided defining it, and now he was gone.

"Who was the hottest?" asked Ateş.

"You, of course," I said.

He smiled and rolled his eyes. "Of course. What a charmer."

We laid on our backs and closed our eyes. I felt like a mischievous, fidgety child trying to fall asleep. Our hands brushed against one another from time to time. Before he drifted into sleep, he grabbed my hand once and held it for a few seconds before he let it go. During that brief moment, I opened my eyes and gazed at the swirling decorative reliefs surrounding the light fixture hanging from the white ceiling of this old Istanbul apartment.

As he slept, I thought back to the men I'd had sex with after Cengiz. A drunk guy who stared at me at the urinals pulled me into the toilet stall at the Kemancı rock bar. Another approached me in the park and led me to a secluded spot in Gezi Park. A fellow student I'd never met before kept eyeing me through the books in the library stacks and followed me to a windowless study room. We all were into sex like indulging in our favorite food together after we've been starved, yet we kept quiet about it and rarely spoke to or saw one another again. Neither our families nor our friends knew, so none of us was *gey*. I fell asleep as I wondered how it'd be with Ateş, especially since he was considering going overseas.

I was taking a graduate seminar in Greco-Roman art that spring semester. While Nesrin *Hanım*, the department head, taught both classes, Oktay, her assistant, subbed for her from time to time when she was away for a conference. I had heard that he was *eşcinsel*, and his appearance seemingly confirmed it: faded jeans with holes around the knees, a sporty top that revealed his skinny arms and shaved chest with newly sprouting hair, metal-framed glasses, and silver stud earrings. But the most telltale sign was a mini braid he wore down his nape, which contrasted with his otherwise bald head. From this hairstyle was born his nickname: *Kılkuyruk,* a pintail—someone who was weak, cowardly, or crafty.

Oktay's lectures were always more engaging than those taught by Nesrin *Hanım,* who gave the impression that she was teaching her courses for the millionth time. But my classmates still laughed at him behind his back—and sometimes to his face.

The week after my encounter with Ateş, Nesrin *Hanım* was at the Twenty-Fifth Annual Association of Art Historians Conference in Rome. Oktay clicked through slides of homoerotic Greek pottery depicting men fighting, bathing, and drinking as he talked, with arms akimbo, about homosexuality in ancient Greek and Roman culture.

"The ancients didn't have a concept of *eşcinsellik* or *homoseksüellik* like we have today. But, of course, as these ceramics show, intimacy between men was quite widespread and acceptable to a certain extent in both cultures. Like it was during the Ottoman Empire later, and perhaps even today," he said and winked.

When he switched to Roman sculptures of wrestlers and hunters, he pointed at the screen and said, "You must've noticed that the bodies depicted in these sculptures are all perfect. I'm sure most people didn't look like demigods back then; there must have been fat, old, or ailing people among the glorious ancients, too, right?"

"Stop, you're ruining it," said a woman's voice from the back row.

A few people giggled.

"Well, this is art imitating life partially and selectively," he said. "Artists tend to depict the world more beautifully than it actually is. Keep in mind, reality is always messier."

I saw a classmate in front of me elbow the guy next to him; another behind me whispered, "He should know," and snorted.

The next day, Ateş and I were to meet for lunch. I rode the crowded municipal bus to Etiler, the neighborhood where he interned at an interior design firm. I watched my reflection in the window as I stood and gripped a hard plastic handle attached to the metal bar overhead. I made some effort to look attractive. My gelled hair was spiky, and I wore a yellow muscle T-shirt that bunched at my armpits and stretched around my shoulders. Sweat was beginning to dampen the fabric in the late spring heat, and my T-shirt was riding up, threatening to bare my midriff. I brought my arm down and switched to the handle attached to the side of a nearby seat.

I got out at Akmerkez, a luxury shopping mall. A large banner above the glass and steel entrance announced that the mall had been voted the best in Europe several times. Many of the Turkish top-1-percenters lived in the area and ate and shopped on Nispetiye Street, where global brands had luxury stores that were air-conditioned, a creature comfort reserved for the rich in 1990s Turkey.

We met in the soaring atrium of Akmerkez. After we hugged, Ateş proposed that we eat at a Chinese restaurant—I'd never been to one before.

It seemed Etiler's business elite also had made plans to lunch at Paper Moon. I was dressed cheaply in my muscle top and blue jeans, like the rent boys who looked for clients in Gezi Park in Taksim.

The hostess seated us by the wall and left us with two oversized menus. There were so many dishes I'd never heard of, and they cost at least three times as much as I'd pay at a local Turkish restaurant. As I read the descriptions and the corresponding prices, I remembered how Ali had teased Ateş by calling him *tiki*.

Ateş placed an order for a dish called "Seafood Birdsnest" and I for General Tso's chicken and rice. I didn't know who this particular general was or whether he had to wage war for his meal, but chicken and rice seemed safe among the otherwise foreign menu items.

All the tables were occupied, and waiters shuttled between the kitchen and the dining area. We faced one another as we sipped our ice water. I pulled and adjusted the armpits of my shirt.

"Our time together was hot," he said.

"Yes, yes," I said as I looked around to make sure no one had heard.

Two bearded business types were sitting at the table next to us. Ateş nodded in their direction and said, "How handsome are they?"

I let out a noncommittal, "I suppose," and concluded that it was all wrong: I was inappropriately dressed and not his type.

"How's school?" he asked.

"It's good. I'm working on a project for my art history class. You?"

"I'm dealing with a customer who is very picky. She's not satisfied with the different designs we proposed for her apartment, and she keeps changing her mind," he said.

A clean-shaven waiter with angular chin and salt-and-pepper hair brought our food. After he left, Ateş said, "He's pretty hot for an older guy, don't you think?"

He was, so I said, "Yes."

We started eating. Ateş picked at his salad, and I tried my General Tso's chicken. The chunks of breaded chicken smothered in tangy, russet sauce with orange rinds tasted good but burned my mouth a little. Chasing them with white rice soothed my tongue. I wondered if Ateş would keep commenting on other men.

"What's your project on?" he asked.

"I'm comparing the Greek and Roman representations of the pantheon in art."

"Gods?"

"Yes."

The two businessmen at the next table got up and left. Ateş turned around and watched them leave. "I don't know if I can handle both," he said and laughed.

I tried to laugh it off, but inside I felt warm, my blood simmering like magma beneath the surface.

"Are you interested in a specific god?" he asked, returning to the topic of my project.

"Yes, the god of fire."

"You are obsessed with me!"

I decided to humor him and said, "Guilty as charged."

He smiled broadly. "Speaking of us, did Arzu know about you?"

"She saw me drunk kiss a guy at Kemancı once. Why?"

"She called me and asked what was going on between us—apparently, she saw us lying next to each other early that morning before we woke up. So, I told her."

"What did she say?"

"She said you always talk about men and never about women."

"I guess I do," I said. "This means Ali knows about us, too."

"Of course. You don't mind, do you?"

"I don't. If I'd have anyone know, it's them," I said.

"Good," he said.

When we finished eating, he checked his watch and said he had to go back to work. He paid the bill, ignoring my protests, and we headed out.

I walked him back to work. We didn't talk about the men we both eyeballed on the way, which was just as well after the restaurant. Before we parted ways, I asked, "Would you like to come with me to the old city to visit a couple of museums on Saturday?"

"I like that idea. We could be tourists for the day, and you could tell me more about this god of fire," he said.

"Your wish is my command," I said.

We hugged and kissed on the cheeks. The passing socialites didn't pay attention to us and continued clacking in their high heels on the sidewalk.

After we parted ways, I took the bus to Bağcılar, where I was renting a converted studio apartment from a retired couple who lived on the second floor of their two-story house. It was very cheap compared to Beşiktaş and close to *otogar,* the municipal depot, where I could catch a bus to my hometown, Çorlu, to visit my parents two hours away.

When I exited the bus in Bağcılar, I aimlessly walked the sidewalks for an hour. It was hot, but I no longer cared about the sweat soaking my T-shirt. Bağcılar, a sleepy, working-class suburb, had a name that meant "vineyard keepers," though the vineyards had surrendered to urban development long ago. Nondescript apartment buildings dominated the neighborhood. Kids played in barren playgrounds or on the sidewalks under windows or balconies from which their stay-at-home mothers, some in conservative headscarves in muted colors and others in colorful kerchiefs, watched as they knitted or hung the laundry to dry. The sound of pop or *arabesk* music issued through open windows, the scenes inside rendered silhouettes by lace curtains. The music would be halted in piety whenever the azan blared from the neighborhood mosque's minarets, unlike in Etiler, where the dominant soundtrack was Western pop and it would never be turned off.

On Saturday, we met in Sultan Ahmet Square in the old city. I wore blue denim shorts and an untucked green T-shirt. Ateş was dressed in beige fabric shorts and a white seersucker shirt, with a brown fedora and black sunglasses to shield his face from the sun. His complexion was pale with sunblock. He looked so much like a foreigner that we got accosted by children who peddled touristy knick-knacks in the square and addressed us in their limited yet effective street English.

"You weren't joking when you said you'd be a tourist," I said.

"I kept my word. What about you?"

"I just wanted to be comfortable."

"Don't you like not being yourself sometimes?"

His outfit reminded me of Harrison Ford in *Indiana Jones,* minus the whip, so I said, "Professor Jones, shall we go forth and see what we can learn from the serpentine column over there about the treasure we seek?"

"Yes, my trusted native friend," Ateş said, "Lead the way, and don't worry, I'm not afraid of snakes anymore."

The remnants of the civilizations that claimed the city were all around us. The boundaries of the Byzantine hippodrome of Constantinople circled three ancient monuments—the Egyptian Obelisk of Theodosius, the Greek Serpent Column, and the Column of Constantine—in the middle of the square. We peered up at them as we shielded our eyes from the scorching sun. The Ottoman Blue Mosque and the Greek Hagia Sophia, the Eastern Roman Orthodox cathedral-turned-mosque-turned-museum, overlooked the square from its opposite ends.

As we surveyed the landscape, *faith* and *resilience* were the words that came to mind, since these structures had stood the test of time in this coveted yet earthquake-prone city. I wondered about the everyday human drama that must've taken place in their shadows, the ephemeral passions that rocked people's hearts before they were swept under the rubble of the endless succession of imperial and military victories these structures were intended to commemorate.

"Can you imagine the conversations people must've had here over the centuries?" I said.

"Not only that, but they also probably frolicked in togas as they were having them!" said Ateş.

"We'll see plenty of that in the museum," I said.

"That's what I'm hoping," said Ateş.

We continued walking through the square toward Istanbul Arkeoloji Müzesi. The museum was an imposing neoclassical building, complete with Greek columns and porticos. The Ottoman imperial seal was placed at the middle of each portico as a reminder of who had been in power when the museum was built. Once inside, we were plunged into a heathen world of ancient Greek and Roman gods, goddesses, and warriors. The air conditioning and nudity blew away the doldrums of the lazy afternoon outside.

"How beautiful and *gey* were they?" said Ateş.

"Well," I started, remembering Oktay's lectures, "they weren't *gey,* and they weren't all bodybuilders, either."

"How do you know?"

"Because I'm studying to become an art historian."

"Just play along," he said and moved on to the next room of the gallery. He stopped to read the plaque in front of another giant marble sculpture. "Hephaestus? Does that sound familiar?" he asked.

"Yes. Funny you ask about that one. That's the Greek god of fire."

"Impressive," he said as he took in the towering figure: A bearded, middle-aged man who wore a sleeveless tunic and a cap over his shaggy hair was fashioning a trident for Poseidon and a spear for Athena.

"Hephaestus is the Greek name for Vulcan. Romans adapted the Greek gods and renamed them. Hephaestus became Vulcan," I said.

He moved on to the next sculpture. "And here's Vulcan," he said as he took in the muscular sculpture that struck an inviting pose, with its right foot propped on a step. A finely carved toga hung from one shoulder across its chiseled chest, covering one nipple and baring the other; the right hand gripped the handle of a hammer while the left hand held a wrench. The toga extended to just above the left knee, while a slit exposed the right thigh all the way to the hip. "I prefer Vulcan. He seems younger and hotter. Don't you think?"

"*Hayır*, I prefer Hephaestus. He was the son of Zeus and Hera, but because he was born lame, his disgusted mother cast him out from Mt. Olympus."

"Needlessly tragic. Is that why you prefer him?"

"No. He was brought back from exile and made weapons and equipment for gods and some mortals, such as Achilles. I guess he had to make himself useful to earn his keep, so I see him as the most humanlike god."

"Relatable. I get it," said Ateş. "But why not enjoy the view, too, you know?"

I rolled my eyes at the unavoidable destination of innuendo in every conversation.

Büyük Saray Mozaikleri Müzesi was a ten-minute walk from the archeological museum, and neither of us had been, so I suggested we stop by. A smaller museum built on the site of the Great Palace of Constantinople, it housed mosaics with scenes from daily life in fifth- and sixth-century Byzantium.

The first set of mosaics depicted animals—a griffin eating a lizard, an elephant and a lion fighting, a mare nursing her foal, bears eating apples. Ateş moved on to the next set, which included people, while I lingered, fascinated by the colors and patterns of the mosaics.

Ateş beckoned me to his side of the gallery and said, "No nudity? Boring. I'll stop by the restroom and find you back here."

I quickly walked through the rest of the museum's main gallery to make our short visit worth the student admission of five liras. A group of kids herded a gaggle of geese, another child fed a donkey, a man milked a goat, a woman carried a clay pot, and a hunter grappled with a lion. They were beautiful in their simplicity, in the way the long-gone anonymous artists' hands arranged disparate pieces of stone into harmonious wholes that have lasted centuries. I was disappointed that Ateş didn't share my appreciation of these depictions.

My impressions of us as a duo were as variegated as the mosaics, but some patterns were emerging.

The following Saturday, we joined Betül, Ateş's female friend, at Baraka, a bar in Beyoğlu, an old cultural and commercial district of Istanbul. Istiklal Street, the main drag, was a shopping mecca during the day. Clothing outlets and bookstores stood side by side with restaurants, and there was an old theater that showed porn, its seedy rows of seats awkward gathering spots for men, straight and *gey*. The neighborhood became a destination for dining and dancing at night, and trans sex workers could be seen walking the streets late at night.

Baraka was located in one of the old buildings continuously lining the main drag. It was on the second floor that jutted out about a meter over the storefront of a buffet-style restaurant. As we approached from the bustling street, we saw multicolored lights flashing on the bar's ceiling and through the windows.

Once inside, we ascended a narrow staircase. The familiar, youthful voice of pop star Ajda Pekkan greeted us singing *"Sana Neler Edeceğim,"* "You'll See What I'll Do to You," her famous song from the '70s, remixed with Western club beats.

The club was converted from an apartment; its former drawing room had tables and chairs on one side and a bar and an open area for dancing on the other. A mixed crowd of men and women moved to the beats, while a few people were gathered at the tables or sipped their drinks at the bar.

Betül was dancing with a man who had a beard and wore his long black hair in a ponytail and a woman with a pixie cut that accentuated her green eyes. Ateş waved at them, and we joined them on the dance floor. The music was so loud that none of us bothered with anything beyond the salutatory *merhaba* and *memnun oldum*. Betül eyeballed me top to bottom and giggled, yelling something into Ateş's ear. She wore a pink strapless blouse over a blue miniskirt; her bangs covered her forehead all the way to her eyebrows, while her otherwise long brown hair with highlights spilled over her bare shoulders.

I wasn't much of a dancer, so I gestured to the bar and left the floor to get myself a drink. Ateş ran behind me, pinched my butt to get my attention, and handed me his cell phone, yelling into my ear, "Could you hold my *cep telefonu*? I don't want to drop it."

I nodded and put the phone in the breast pocket of my black button-up shirt. After grabbing an Efes beer at the bar, I took a seat at a corner table. I nursed my beer and wondered if the people in the club, especially the guys, saw him pinching me, and what they thought. The table under my elbow and the floor under my feet vibrated.

Several songs later, Ateş and his friends came over to my corner table. Pixie Cut sat on the lap of Bearded Ponytail, and they started making out.

Betül didn't sit. She wiped her eyes and grabbed her bag. I wondered if it was the cigarette smoke or real tears.

"What happened?" I asked Ateş.

"Boyfriend drama. They've been having sex, but he seems less and less interested in her. They might break up."

Her old-fashioned name reminded me of classic Turkish movies with rich, bratty female leads.

"What's going to happen when the next guy finds out?" I asked.

"Finds out what?" he said.

"That she's not *bakire*."

Ateş gave me a surprised look and said, "If he cares about her hymen, then he's not the right guy for her." He stood up, put his arm around Betül, and guided her toward the bar.

Ateş and Betül led lives very different from mine in the suburbs, where an unmarried woman was expected to preserve her virginity until marriage. I watched my parents regulate my sisters' lives as I grew up. One's location clearly made a big difference, and I felt foolish. I sipped my beer and watched the tiny bubbles rise to the surface.

Around midnight, Ateş and I left Baraka. The couple was dancing to slow music, and Betül was chatting with a man at the bar. Ateş saw that I still had his phone in my left breast pocket. He grabbed it and said with dramatic flair, "What if this phone gave you a heart attack or something? I'd never forgive myself."

This was long before mobile phones became sleek and smart. We didn't know what effect clunky cell phones like Ateş's Ericsson would have on us exactly, and Y2K loomed large on the horizon.

I laughed at his comment and said, "I'm fine." I was pleasantly buzzed and relieved to finally have his full attention.

We took a taxi from Taksim to Ateş's home in Emirgan, a historic hillside neighborhood overlooking the Bosphorus Strait. Ateş had told me that his parents were in their vacation home in Bodrum on the Aegean coast.

Ali did have good reason to call Ateş *tiki*. When we arrived at their fourth-floor apartment, the contemporary foyer with its sleek parquet floor made me feel like we were entering an apartment featured in a design magazine. The spacious living room, which we stopped in on the way to his bedroom, was tastefully furnished, without ostentation, and had a direct view of the strait and the imposing Fatih Sultan Mehmet suspension bridge spanning the waterway in the distance.

After I took in the view, we moved to his bedroom. A book on interior design was left open on his desk among a stack of other books, pencils, a sketchpad, and a paperweight with swirling colors of the rainbow, so the room had more of a feel that someone lived there. We hugged each other as the city and the bridge hummed outside.

Ateş pushed me onto his full-sized bed, laid on top of me, and kissed me deeply. I stroked his back and slid my hand down the back of his pants as he rubbed against me. We unzipped one another and kicked off our pants. Having sex with him on his bed, in his family's home, was so arousing that it didn't take us long to climax.

Our breathing returned to normal as we laid on our backs beside each other. I looked around and saw pictures on the walls and his night-stand that portrayed his changing good looks from childhood to the present. His parents were with him in a few of the pictures. They seemed proud of their only child.

"Do your parents know?" I asked.

"Do yours?" he replied.

Okay, there was nothing to talk about there.

"I'll tell you who my first crush was, if you tell me yours," he said.

"It was the son of the grocery store owner. I was twelve, and he was fourteen."

"Mine was my boss," he said.

"What, your current boss? How old is he?"

"Yes. He just turned fifty but looks much younger. He's been a family friend for years, and he offered me the internship. I even told him how I felt last year."

"You did not. How?"

"We were in Milan for a design fair. At the end of the day, we were sitting at a bar, and I got too drunk, so I told him that I loved him."

"*Allah'ım,* what did he say?"

"He talked about how it wasn't right, that he was married. Expected, but you know what I didn't expect? He still wanted to fuck me. As if I was just a piece of meat."

"Not surprising, considering how cute you are. And older men have always gotten their way with younger men here." I thought of male *köçek* dancers who entertained older men during Ottoman times. "Did you do it?"

"No. As soon as we were back in the hotel room he had booked for the trip, he grabbed me and tried to kiss me. When I pulled away, he was like, 'What's the big deal? I thought you loved me.' I cried quietly most of the night in my bed. He snored in his bed as if nothing happened."

A long-suppressed sob worked its way up his torso.

"I'm sorry," I said and hugged him. "You have to leave that job."

"I can't. My parents know him. They got me the job. I can't just quit. That's why I want to go away, do a master's in England or something. I've been going to therapy to deal with it."

This was the first time he was real with me—no jokes, no frivolity. But now that he told me he loved someone else, what did that mean for us?

After that weekend, I didn't see Ateş for a week or so. He was away in Bodrum with his parents. I went back to the museums, took pictures and notes, and spoke to curators for my research. I found out that pre-Roman Italian gods were not anthropomorphic. Originally an elemental deity of fire, Vulcan became more humanlike when the Romans adopted the blacksmith characteristics of the Greek Hephaestus; however, they continued associating Vulcan with fertility—they used volcanic ash as fertilizer—and with destructiveness. They held a Vulcanalia festival in the summer in his honor and sacrificed fish and other small animals by throwing them into bonfires to appease him.

Ateş called a few times when I was visiting my parents in Çorlu. Heading into my mid-twenties and being nearly finished with my studies, I was at a marriageable age. The first time we spoke on our home landline, its long cord stretching from the hallway to my room, my mother was hopeful.

"Is that *gelinim* calling?" she asked as she rinsed flour off her hands in the kitchen sink. She must have finished the *börek* she was making.

I rolled my eyes at her suggestion that it was a prospective daughter-in-law on the line.

"No, it's my friend Ateş from college."

She looked deflated as she shook her wet hands over the sink.

"When will you bring us a *gelin?*"

"I have several beautiful candidates I'm managing at the moment," I said as I passed her the kitchen towel.

She smiled, but immediately transitioned to death-and-duty mode, "*Canım,* I want to see your *mürüvet* before I die. My Allah-given task as a parent is not over until then. Don't make me go to my grave with eyes open!"

"*Aman anne,*" I said, "you must be watching old Turkish movies again. Plus, you look as young as me and will probably bury me."

She slapped me on the shoulder and said, "*Sus,* it's *günah* to say such things, and that would be a real tragedy! Now, go get me more eggs from the *bakkal.* I need two more to finish the *börek.*"

"*Tamam,* I'll make sure to hang on until after you go," I said and kissed her on the cheek, despite her protestations, before I left the kitchen.

My military officer father also asked about women, but he assumed that I was having sex. His generation of Turkish men thought that any women were game if they weren't married. He'd ask, "So, who was that girl who said hi to you on the street the other day? Are you sleeping with her?" If I said no, he'd say, "Why not?" He'd advise me to use *prezervatif* to avoid catching STDs and getting them pregnant, but would contradict himself and warn me that fornication was *günah.*

The mention of sin would bring us to marriage. Was I seeing anyone seriously? He would tell me to be careful and find an *iyi aile kızı,* a virtuous woman from a good family.

I wondered if and how I could come out to them, but it seemed out of the question for now, so I kept my mouth shut. They would take me to a doctor or an imam, or both. So we continued playing *saklambaç,* simultaneously hiding and seeking.

After he returned from the Aegean coast, I called Ateş to invite him to the School of Fine Arts' end-of-the-semester social on campus. He immediately said yes. I was excited that he was coming but also nervous because I didn't know what this meant for us and what it would signal to my classmates who'd meet him in such a public setting.

I stopped by Ali's that afternoon to study. He was working on a term paper, and I was studying for my finals. Ever the hospitable host, he made coffee for us. Since I had hooked up with Ateş in his apartment, every act of hospitality somehow felt like a tacit endorsement. I told him that Ateş would be joining us at the social on campus. I wasn't asking his permission, but I still wanted to gauge his reaction.

Ali put down his coffee mug, cleared his throat, and said, "Don't bring him."

"Why not?" I said.

"You know, Gökhan, I don't have a problem with the two of you," said Ali, "but think about what happens after graduation. Others will wonder and eventually figure it out. You don't want to endanger your future."

"I don't care," I said.

"*Tamam,* it's your business," he said and returned to his final project about the fine arts market in Turkey.

I should have listened to him, but not for the reasons he mentioned.

The gathering was held on the promenade in front of the old campus building on the shore of the Bosphorus, with a direct view of the old city where we had visited the museums in the distance, and the Maiden's Tower closer to the Üsküdar shore across the strait. The evening sea breeze with a briny scent caressed our faces as we arrived.

Ali and Arzu waved at us from where they were dancing and pointed at the cash bar. We got in line for drinks. Tolga joined the line behind us. Ateş saw him and nudged me before he turned around and said hi. He had a big smile on his face, like a kid who had just spotted his new favorite toy. Tolga told us that he booked his first television commercial, so I listened to Ateş compliment Tolga as if he were a film star, telling him he wasn't surprised. Tolga, who seemed used to such compliments, smiled politely. Thankfully, we soon reached the front of the line. We grabbed a couple of beers and moved on to say hi to Ali and Arzu. As we caught up with our friends, I saw Ateş watch Tolga as he headed in the opposite direction to mingle with his friends.

As the night went on and we kept drinking, Ateş, who didn't carry his alcohol well, began following Tolga through the dancing crowd like a puppy.

I spent nearly an hour trying to distract him and pull him away and get him sobered up—I even stood beside him as he vomited in the restroom stall and cleaned him up after.

I had introduced Ateş as my friend to many of my classmates at the beginning of the evening; now that they witnessed our drama, they probably doubted my account of us. It was embarrassing, and I was jealous, which made me even more upset.

When we returned to the party, with Ateş leaning on me as we walked, Arzu asked if he was okay. Ali gave me an I-told-you-so look. I nodded and left Ateş in their care to grab some water and napkins.

When I returned, I saw Ateş, who now sat on the floor, spit into his hands and wipe drops of vomit from his shoes. I couldn't help it anymore, so I said, "Disgusting!"

He looked up and shouted, "If I'm so disgusting, Gökhan, then don't sleep with me!"

Everyone nearby heard and understood who he really was to me. I grabbed him by the forearm, led him outside, and hailed a taxi without saying goodbye to anyone.

I didn't say a word on the way, and Ateş was passed out for most of the ride to Emirgan. I watched the city fly by as we rode on the highway over the hills of Istanbul.

We arrived at his parents' apartment twenty minutes later. Fortunately, they were still away. When we went to his room, he attempted to kiss me, but I just couldn't. His breath smelled sour. Instead, I gave him a quick hand job. It was a feeble attempt to set things right. His desire made me forget everything for the moment. As he trembled and came in my arms, he looked flushed and vulnerable.

He fell asleep almost immediately, which made me feel used. In the midnight quiet, I saw myself as an intruder in the apartment. I looked around his room; his parents smiled from the frames on the wall. I didn't know them, but I envied their old age and the seeming lack of drama in their lives. I thought of what happened tonight and knew it was all wrong.

I dreamt I was a blacksmith. Against a sooty background lit up by a great fire, I held down Ateş with pliers and hammered at him to mold him into a desirable shape. My face showed effort and frustration, and sweat dripped onto my beard. The more I hammered, the more misshapen he became, until he was unrecognizable. I woke up sweating and instantly understood what I needed to do. It made me sad to look at Ateş, who slept next to me like a baby.

In the morning, we walked quietly down to the coastal road by the Bosphorus, where I was to catch my bus back home.

When we arrived at the bus stop, Ateş said, "We should eat breakfast first. You can catch the next one." He seemed groggy, and a lick of hair stood up at the back of his head.

"I have work to do," I said. The real reason was that I'd never broken up with someone I cared about. If I stayed more, I didn't think I could do it.

"I'm sorry about last night. I shouldn't have drunk so much," said Ateş.

"I tried to stop you, but it was too late, you wouldn't listen."

He was quiet.

I said, "I can't be with you anymore. It's best if we break this off, whatever it is."

He looked at me and said, "You used me, and now you're throwing me away."

This was a classic breakup line from old Turkish movies. I couldn't help but smile as my eyes watered. I realized he was tearing up, too.

I swallowed the knot in my throat and said, "Do you remember following Tolga around? Yelling at me in front of my classmates?"

"A little," said Ateş and wiped his eyes.

I could go into more detail but didn't want to. I said, "I'm sorry, I can't do this."

My bus turned the corner in the distance. We hugged one last time. He said he wanted to stay in touch. I said I would, but knew I wouldn't.

I boarded the bus and walked to the standing area at the back, where I could see Ateş through the window.

We waved at each other.

As the bus took me away, he kept looking my way but got smaller and smaller. He finally disappeared from my view.

I watched the tire tracks on the asphalt road. The morning heat was already melting the tar on its surface.

RUNWAY

Hasan came to consider himself more of a *seks işçisi* than a "rent boy" after he started attending the events of Gökkuşağı Ağı, the Rainbow Network. The organization's office was a converted two-bedroom flat on the third floor of an old apartment building in the Alsancak neighborhood of Izmir on the Aegean coast of Turkey. At first, he felt completely out of place. It seemed the meetings took the fun out of being gay, with their earnest talk about rights and whatnot, but there were free condoms and food, which made it worth listening to some *çok bilmiş beyaz yakalı* for an hour. And occasionally, those white-collar know-it-alls were interested in more than conversation.

He met others there who called themselves *seks işçisi* activists. They talked about their—and his—rights as a sex worker. He liked this label because it demanded respect. Also, despite his still boyish looks—he was now thirty-two—who could call himself a rent boy forever when those looks could last only so long? He was in the market for a *şugar baba* for the short or long term and made that known whenever the opportunity presented itself.

This Friday's event was titled "Amerika'da Eşcinsel Evlilik Aktivizmi," "Same-Sex Marriage Activism in the United States." Hasan was fashionably late, as usual. When he walked in the front door, he could hear a man speaking English with an American accent in the meeting room. The session was clearly under way, so he ducked into the kitchen and poured himself some hot black *çay,* the beverage staple at such events, from the twin kettles on the range—the smaller one, with the infused tea, sitting on top of the bigger one, with simmering hot water and steam emanating from its spout—before joining the group. There were a couple dozen attendees, men and women, sitting on white plastic chairs arranged in a circle, an easel with paper at the corner, and a table full of food along with some less appetizing brochures about STDs. The windows overlooking the side street had no curtains and the cream-colored walls were bare, except for a few posters for upcoming parties and drag performances and a bulletin board tacked with colorful fliers and festooned with pictures from past Pride Weeks. The first Pride March in Turkey was held in Istanbul in 2003, a year after the ruling Adalet ve Kalkınma Partisi (AKP, Justice and Development Party) first came to power in 2002. During the seven years since the first Istanbul Pride, celebrations had spread to Izmir and other cities across Turkey, but LGBT activists remained wary of AKP's pro-Islamist stance, especially after Minister Selma Aliye Kavaf of Women and Family Affairs declared homosexuality a "disease" and stated her opposition to same-sex marriage in 2010.

Hasan was wearing tight black denim shorts and a sleeveless lavender muscle shirt that hugged his thin frame—it was cut so narrowly that it barely covered his nipples. As he looked for an empty seat, he felt all eyes on him, including those of the guest speaker, who was quiet for a moment and cleared his throat. Hasan's long lashes over soft green eyes and *elma yanaklar ve kiraz dudaklar*—apple cheeks and cherry lips—had always commanded the attention of some men, who found his seeming innocence enticing. But the men with money were older and had wives, and they wouldn't tell what they wanted—a woman with a dick or simply a man—until in bed. So he had recently grown *kirli sakal,* a short beard, and put on a bit of a swagger, cultivating mixed or, in the academic lingo at the network, *kuir* signals to cover as broad a frequency of tastes as possible.

Hasan dropped his Puma duffel bag, which had a change of clothes just in case, on the side of his chair as he steadied his teacup. When he looked up at the speaker, he saw that the rectangular sticker on his left pectoral said *ADAM* in what looked like a child's handwriting. He was a tall as a minaret, blond, blue-eyed American with a Roman nose, a cleft chin, and broad shoulders. He looked like he was in his forties. Hasan put his tea on the floor and immediately texted Mehmet, his best buddy and roommate, "*Kız, bu Amerikalı koli çok şugar!*" They addressed each other as *girl* as a joke. Mehmet was a former rent boy with brown hair and a slightly pockmarked face he felt compelled to cover with foundation. He now lived off potbellied Sezgin, a rich *müteahhit* in the construction business who was married with four kids; Mehmet referred to himself as the man's *metres*—his mistress. He hated email and disliked talking on the phone, but was a chatterbox in person and was trigger-happy when it came to *güllüm* through texting. He shot back a thumbs-up and an emoji with dollars for eyes and on the tongue. The arriving text pinged and elicited a disapproving look from the butch lesbian across the room. Hasan sighed and silenced his phone begrudgingly.

Hasan had met Mehmet five years ago in the nearby Kültürpark, famous for the Izmir Enternasyonal Fuarı, the annual commercial and cultural fair. The park was also Izmir's cruising spot, its open secret in the middle of town. On an unusually quiet midsummer evening in 2005, they happened to sit on the same bench and ended up trading stories about the weird men they'd slept with. A good-looking man in a suit approached and struck up a conversation. Osman turned out to be a real estate lawyer visiting out of town and looking for a quick release without wrinkling or soiling his clothes. He needed to rush to a formal business dinner at the historic Asansör building, named after the fifty-one-meter-high elevator tower built over a hundred years ago. The restaurant at the top had a spectacular view of the Aegean shoreline. He took Hasan and Mehmet to his room at the Hilton Izmir and paid a hundred lira to watch them. As they pretended to have passionate sex, he pleasured himself. Afterward, Hasan and Mehmet went to a nearby *büfe* and joked as they devoured chicken gyro sandwiches. Mehmet declared they were now officially *kızkardeşler,* sisters, which sealed their close friendship forever. Within a few months, they became roommates, and they had looked out for each other ever since.

Hasan enjoyed watching Adam, but listening to him speak English was distracting. It made him feel like a tennis player who swung wildly but hit only one out of every five balls launched toward him. The English he had picked up on the street, and practice, lots of it, with English-speaking men allowed him to get paid in dollars. Who cared if his pronunciation wasn't perfect or he missed a few words? He could get his point across, and in situations he couldn't, he relied on the power of body language. During Adam's talk, however, he had to remind himself of the Turkish title of the event and tried to catch his meaning from words he recognized like *gey* marriage, *aktivizm, kongre, senato,* and *lobi.* Adam gestured enthusiastically and went on about the topic.

Hasan looked around. Did everyone really understand what Adam was saying? And did everyone really want to get married? In Hasan's experience, sex work and marriage were like two sisters who acted like the other didn't exist. He remembered the countless married men who had turned gay in his hands. The thought made him chuckle. Adam looked at him and smiled.

Emboldened by Adam's smile, Hasan raised his hand during the Q&A and parroted a line he had heard others say during network meetings before: "*Gey* marriage? Not fan because no room for people like me."

Adam blinked and asked, "Why not?"

"Sex work. I asked a sugar daddy from," he fumbled for English words and gave up, "Çalışma ve Sosyal Güvenlik Bakanlığı."

A few people in the audience laughed. Hasan was pleased that they got his joke. The moderator rolled his eyes and translated, "The Ministry of Labor and Social Security." Adam laughed, too, but before he could respond, the moderator ended the Q&A, saying, "Why don't we continue the discussion over the reception?"

Hasan snapped his fingers and said, "Yes, hungry."

Hasan hovered around the food table and scarfed multiple pieces of *dolma* and *sigara böreği* from aluminum foil containers. He watched Adam from a distance. White-collar gays who were probably all university students or graduates mobbed Adam like bees to honey. Their questions might've been about activism and gay marriage, but they all wanted to get into his pants.

Adam, the marriage guy, wasn't wearing a ring—not that it would stop Hasan. As he eyeballed him from head to toe, he thought of a Turkish saying about a woman who doesn't show her age: *Minare yıkılmış ama mihrab yerinde*, "the minaret is down but the mihrab is still in place." The absurdity of applying such a traditional saying to Adam made him giggle. At that point, Hasan saw Adam glance his way. He suppressed his laugh so that he wouldn't look like a crazy person. He licked the oil off his index finger suggestively as he pretended to read the dietary label of his sweetened iced tea. It was a good sign that Adam was still giving him the eye; he took Hasan's bait during the Q&A.

Hasan relished the prospect of finding out who this guy really was. It was his favorite aspect of being a sex worker. Sometimes he would run into a regular *müşteri*, and the man would pretend he didn't know him in public, but Hasan knew all about him and what got him hot and bothered. That inside knowledge was more arousing than sex itself— and once or twice that kind of closeness was what made him fall for a trick, despite Mehmet's warnings not to mix business and emotions. He couldn't help it, especially when the deal was not a quickie but an extended pretense of being a part of a new man's life, like being tele- ported into another existence. If he liked that life better, he didn't want to come back to his own. This was why Mehmet teased him about being a *romantik,* and on rare occasions, he was guilty as charged.

After the event, the group walked to the Cix Club for drinks. The gay bar had a rooftop patio lit with lanterns that cast a rosy hue. Hasan and Adam sat across from each other at the elongated table for their group of fifteen. People chattered in Turkish as they debated in small groups how US activism might or might not work in Turkey. Hasan jostled the ice in his Diyet Kola with his plastic straw and watched as Adam smoked, drank his *rakı* like it was beer, and nodded at the college guy in cargo shorts and a Captain America T-shirt who was happy to show off his English to an American. The college guy had spent a semester in New York and wouldn't shut up about it, referring to America as "the States." Hasan would've probably spoken English better than this kid, like a European even, if his parents hadn't dragged him from Bulgaria to Turkey when he was a few years old. In fact, his whole life would've unfolded differently, but it was no use thinking about that now. He scratched between the middle and ring fingers of his left hand, where his skin bore the marks of the botched plastic surgery that carved out the webbing there.

Hasan texted Mehmet, "*Cix kulübdeyiz. Ismi Adam!*"

Mehmet texted back immediately, "*Adem? Sen de Havva'sın o zaman!*"

As Hasan cracked up at the thought of being Adam's Eve, Adam looked at him and leaned forward.

"What should I see in Izmir? I'm new here," said Adam.

"Karşıyaka, my home, on the other side of water," said Hasan and added, "Ephesus if you abandoned Izmir." His past foreign tricks had raved about it.

"What if I get lost?" said Adam.

"I'm your guide," said Hasan.

"We should do that. You're hired," said Adam.

They clinked their glasses. Hasan watched Adam down half his glass of *rakı*. He chased it with another drag on his cigarette without taking his eyes off Hasan.

The pretense of a local showing around a foreigner who didn't speak Turkish was a necessary cover in Hasan's line of work. Sex work was legal in registered brothels that employed women in Turkey, but it was criminal otherwise. If caught by the police, he could be detained, fined, or even beaten—as he was once—so Hasan had to be careful, to not let himself be humiliated that way ever again.

For the rest of the night, Adam was *çantada keklik,* a partridge in a bag. When Adam offered to share a taxi, Hasan knew he wasn't going home. They arrived at the Swissotel Büyük Efes in downtown Izmir. Unlike in lesser hotels, where the front desk would question two men of dubious connection, five-star places like this one turned a blind eye. Hasan followed Adam's tipsy beckoning to the elevator under the gaze of hotel staff who smiled and said, "*Hoş geldiniz.*" Good thing Hasan only had Diyet Kola, because Adam needed help finding his room key to swipe in the elevator.

Three years ago, Hasan swore not to drink on the nights he worked. He woke up shivering on the front steps of his building in the early morning after a night of carousing that began with a man offering to buy him a drink. Hasan remembered his breathy voice, and his low-hanging head and toothy grin reminded him of a hyena. He could hardly remember the slightest detail of what had happened beyond that. He stumbled upstairs, wincing with each step and calling for Mehmet. He stripped naked, and they checked his body for bruises. Thank Allah, there weren't any, but his body hurt all over, and his wallet was missing. Mehmet barked at him for putting himself in danger, then hugged him and told him to take a shower. The warm water quieted his shaking hands as he cried. A few months later, he tested positive for HIV. He wept as he viewed his test results and wondered if it was due to that one night or the many nights before with other men.

Hasan was open with Mehmet about everything regarding himself, but he debated if he should tell his friend about his HIV status. He read online how the positive were viewed as a threat to the public, like criminals, and shunned. What if Mehmet didn't want to be his roommate anymore, much less his friend? When he finally told him, Mehmet was upset at first, but like a big sister ready to take on anyone who so much as curled a lip at her baby sis, he was by Hasan's side during his doctor's appointments at the public clinic in the Karşıyaka municipality's Sağlık İşleri Müdürlüğü, the Health Affairs Directorship, and made sure he had his prescriptions filled. It was a huge relief to realize their friendship not only survived, but was stronger. As for his *müşteriler*, he made the mistake of revealing his now undetectable status to a long-term trick he had come to like and trust; the man, who knew that Hasan and his family were Bulgarian immigrants, called him "*Allah'ın belası hastalıklı Bulgar ibnesi*," "Goddamned diseased Bulgarian fag," and kicked him out of the seedy hotel room. As he took the metro home, he broke down sobbing and decided not to divulge it again because he had to eat and pay rent.

As soon as Adam unlocked the hotel room's door, he headed for the bathroom. Hasan sat on the king-sized bed. The white linen felt soft under his hands, and the plush burgundy bed runner pampered the back of his bare legs. He listened to the sound of urine hitting water as he took in his environment. The all-glass front of the spacious room overlooked Körfez, the Gulf of Izmir. Behind his reflection, a few boats and ships blinked in the darkness that stretched from the streetlights along the shoreline below to those in Karşıyaka across the gulf. On the other side of the room were a burgundy suede sofa and armchairs with fluffy gray-and-pink-colored print cushions around a sleek coffee table over gray wall-to-wall carpet. A couple of abstract oil paintings with a color palette of blue, purple, and lavender graced the ivory walls, and a glass chandelier hung from the ceiling. The artificial-looking pink orchids on the bedside tables enhanced the room's sophisticated feel. He reached out and touched a petal; it felt silky and real between his fingers.

On the way from the bathroom to the bed, Adam pulled his navy-blue polo shirt over his head and stripped off his gray khaki pants, baring a lean, freckled body with toned muscles and suntanned, aging skin.

"Your turn," said Adam.

"What?"

"Your clothes. Unless you want me to tear them off you."

"Promise you buy new ones?"

Adam tackled Hasan on the bed and pulled off Hasan's shorts without unbuckling his belt. The cheap faux leather of the belt rubbed against his thighs and left red marks on his skin. Hasan rubbed them to make sure the skin wasn't broken.

"Are you being a wimp?" said Adam.

"Vimp?"

"*Wimp.*" Adam mouthed the word like he was in an instructional video. "Softie?"

"Oh, you not rough enough," said Hasan as he sat up. He took off his lavender shirt and put his arms around Adam's neck. *Gözler kalbin aynasıdır, eyes are the mirror of the heart.* As he stared into his blue irises, Hasan wondered what kind of a heart Adam had. An impulse overtook him. Against his better judgment, he said, "I'm *pozitif.*" He was prepared to grab his clothes and duffel bag and leave the hotel in shame.

"You've been bad," replied Adam with a crooked smile. "I like that. We won't draw blood. I have condoms," he said matter-of-factly in his reassuring nasal accent as he hopped off the bed.

Equal parts relieved and nervous, Hasan pulled the bedsheet over his legs to his waist. He watched Adam retrieve his wallet from his pants on the floor, take out a couple of condoms, and lay them on the nightstand, but instead of coming to bed, he went back to the closet and pulled out a necktie.

"Since we're sharing," said Adam, "would you mind being tied?"

Hasan let the sheet go, kneeled on the bed, extending his hands to Adam with palms facing one another, and said, "Not very tight."

When he woke up early in the morning, Hasan's wrists were sore, and his body felt tingly all over. Those sensations soon gave way to a self-pleased smile for having discovered Adam's sexual predilection and to hunger after seeing that Adam had breakfast delivered to the room. The tray included an omelet—the scent of rosemary wafted from it—black and green olives, feta, diced cucumbers and tomatoes, assorted jams and butter in tiny white bowls, orange juice, and black *çay.*

"Turkish breakfast is the best," said Adam as he brought the tray over to the bed. "So much fiber for regularity." He grinned, flashing bright white teeth. His wet blond hair glistened in the morning light.

Regularity? Hasan didn't know what that meant, so he said, "Glad you like."

"I did give you a workout, didn't I?"

"You chose me and not younger gays for exercise?"

"I liked you better, and I was right," said Adam and winked. "They were nice and cute but also inexperienced and full of expectations. I wanted you, a pro. Cut through the bullshit, you know."

"Yes, no bullshit. Knowed many pros?" Hasan wondered if "pro" was short for "professional" or "prostitute." He considered himself a *profesyonel* but didn't like *prostitute*; it reminded him of *orospu,* a word of shame and disrespect for women in his line of work. The fat policeman had kept calling him that as he beat him up that one time. Words had power, and choosing them was how people wielded it, for better or worse. If he must use a common term, he preferred the less judgmental, if shadowy, *hayat kadını,* a woman of the life. That would make him *hayat adamı,* a man of the life. And today, he was Adam *adamı.*

"A few, but you're my first pro tour guide," said Adam. "Speaking of which, let's go to Ephesus today."

"Okay," said Hasan. "But no cheap."

"I wouldn't expect you to be cheap."

"Five hundred *dolar,* including last night." Mehmet always said that if you didn't bargain, you weren't Turkish, so Hasan always asked for twice as much as he thought he could get.

"That's a steal," said Adam.

Hasan smiled as if he always charged such an amount, but inside he rejoiced; a dollar was worth three Turkish liras, so this was going to be the best deal he had ever had.

Adam pushed the tray aside and leaned on Hasan with all his weight like he wanted to crush him. Hasan contemplated the prospect of a memorable day with Adam; he had enjoyed his company, plus he had never been to Ephesus, so he felt excited about being whisked away to the ancient city. Practical considerations slipped away under Adam's passionate kiss.

Shortly thereafter, Adam called the concierge as Hasan showered and changed. He arranged for them to be picked up in an hour in front of the hotel for the day's tour. While they waited, Hasan texted Mehmet in *lubunca,* a slang mixture of Turkish and Romani he and Mehmet picked up from trans sex workers: "*But similyalı balamozla haftasonu,*" letting him know that he was spending the weekend with the well-endowed

Adam. Mehmet shot back two quick messages: a thumbs-up with two dollar signs, and "*Dikkat kız*"—"Careful, girl." Hasan decided not to tell Mehmet about being tied up to avoid worrying him and getting lectured, and he kept quiet about Ephesus to surprise him later.

After an hour-long *minibüs* ride, their tour arrived in Ephesus late in the morning. The guide led them down Curetes Street among the ruins under the relentless Aegean sun and shared the history of the city, explaining the purpose and architectural significance of the Hercules Gate, the Fountain of Trajan, the Baths of Scholastica, and the Temple of Hadrian. They took a selfie in front of the famous facade of the Library of Celsus; they were surprised to hear that after a fire destroyed the building in the third century, it lay in ruins until it was reconstructed in the 1970s. During a break from the tour, they petted an orange tabby cat lounging on top of the pedestal of a long-gone column and sat on the latrines pretending to be Ephesians.

Adam imitated a British accent and said, "Mate, I can see your cut willy."

Hasan closed his eyes, stretched his hands, and said, "Where are you? The smell of your shit blind me."

Adam punched Hasan's shoulder. The tour guide apparently overheard their crass jokes, because he gave them a sideways glance that seemed to question whether they really were who they said they were. He had asked them during the bus ride how they knew each other. Adam told him that they were coworkers at an import-export company.

Their second stop on the tour was Meryem Ana Evi, the House of the Virgin Mary. According to the tour guide, St. John brought Mary to Ephesus after the passing of Isa, Jesus, and she spent her last days there. The small *L*-shaped shrine was built of stone blocks intercut with worn red bricks. Arches adorned the facade, and there were arched doors and high windows barred with lattice ironwork. Inside were candles for offerings and an altar; the statue of the Virgin stood above the altar in the recess behind it, surrounded with fresh flowers and candles. Down a flight of stairs from the shrine, another arched stone wall held three faucets that dispensed water believed to have curative properties from an underground source called the Water of Mary. Further down the wall was a *dilek duvarı*, where thousands of wishes written on paper or tissues were hung on a trellis that extended along the stonework for at least ten meters.

Hasan didn't go to mosque but believed in Allah. As a testament to their Turkishness, his parents had made him attend the Koran school at the local mosque during summer breaks before he ran away from home at fourteen, so he knew that both *Hazreti* Isa and *Hazreti* Meryem were mentioned in several suras and revered in the Koran. He cupped his hands and drank from the faucets one by one. The saline water burned his throat a little, but he still felt refreshed in the summer heat. He pulled out a crumpled piece of paper—an old receipt—from his pocket, smoothed it out against a stone, and scribbled on the empty back *Allah'ım sağlıklı kalmayı nasip et,* wishing to stay healthy. He glanced at Adam, who was checking his phone in the shade of an olive tree, and decided to add *ve Adam'ı görmeyi*—to see more of Adam. Whatever that would mean. He rolled up the paper and stuck it into a cluster of other wishes on the wall. In addition to his being the best and most accepting customer so far, after last night, they seemed to have such *ten uyumu,* with every touch, intentional or not, stoking their desire for one another, that he couldn't help that second wish. He walked up to Adam and asked, "No wish?"

Adam looked up and said, "I don't believe in that shit."

"Aren't you Hristiyan?"

"Christian? Yes, I was raised Catholic, but I'm an atheist now," said Adam as he put his phone away. "What did you wish?"

"No, can't happen if I tell," said Hasan.

"Right," said Adam and tousled Hasan's hair.

Hasan felt an electrical charge run through his body. He wanted to kiss Adam then and there but wouldn't dare.

Their tour included a *tabildot* lunch at Egelim, a roadside restaurant the tour company contracted to cater to its guests. They waited in line with their lunch trays. Everyone got a small *çoban salatası,* shepherd's salad with diced tomatoes, cucumbers, and onions; four square slices of baklava; and a yogurt drink called *ayran*—beads of water ran down the sides of its plastic cup. There were two options for the main dish: a vegetarian pasta or beef *döner* over white rice. Hasan and Adam couldn't resist the appetite-whetting scent of meat presoaked in marinade and roasted on a sword-like skewer.

Most of the restaurant's seating was outdoors. Picnic tables with flower-patterned plastic covers were scattered around the property, which was adjacent to an orchard. They sat at the table closest to the fruit trees, which were laden with apples, peaches, and pears and defied the noon heat that settled on them like a smothering blanket.

Once they sat and started eating, Hasan said, "Tell me more about Mister *Gey* Marriage."

"Yeah, right," said Adam. "You still call me that after last night? I have to work harder."

"Rest first. We walked hills and valleys," said Hasan. "Now tell me."

"Okay, I'm from Michigan. The northern part, called the Upper Peninsula."

"*Mişigın?*"

"In the Midwest, to the North. Grew up on a farm. Very small town. Snows a ton."

"I like snow, but too warm here."

"You'd hate it if you lived in Michigan."

"Any gays?"

"I thought I was the only one. I got out when I went to college in DC and stayed. What about you?"

"I'm from Çorlu in Trakya. Parents come from Bulgaristan when few years old. Only son. They don't like me *kuir* and beat me for it. So, I ran. You guess the rest."

"Ah, sorry. And yeah, I've definitely found out some of the rest." Adam sipped from his *ayran* and licked his lips.

"You go back to *Mişigın?*"

"I visit for Christmas if I'm still in the country."

"Noel. *Güzel.*"

"What's that?"

"*Güzel.* Means nice—or beautiful for persons." Hasan smiled.

"*Güzel,* then," said Adam.

"I want to be traveling someday," said Hasan.

"Yeah, it's great. I travel a lot now that I have my own international consulting business. Since last year."

"Before that?"

"I worked in Washington, DC, for a nonprofit. We surveyed people about gay marriage and other stuff. Did workshops and talked to local governments about the issue."

"And now spreading it across the earth."

"You make it sound like a space mission," Adam laughed. "It's legal in DC and five states now and will probably become legal in the rest of the country, too, as soon as the Supreme Court takes up the issue."

"But no ring. Why not married?"

"Because I don't fucking believe in marriage."

Hasan tilted his head and raised his eyebrows. "Joke? I don't understand why you do this work."

Adam put his fork down as he chewed the meat. He glanced at the trees and then leaned forward and said, "Why do you sell your *güzel* body?"

"Money. And fun."

"I need to work for a living, too."

"But not the same."

"I don't mean the specifics. We both do what pays and what people want," said Adam and drank from his *ayran*.

"Yes, but why 'I don't fucking believe in marriage'?" said Hasan as he tried to speak through his nose to imitate Adam's accent.

"Are you making fun of me?"

"Maybe. A little." Hasan patted Adam's forearm and grinned.

"I actually was married to a guy. I met Mark through that DC organization. We dated for about six years before marriage became legal in DC."

"Late congratulations," said Hasan.

Adam rolled his eyes and said, "Well, at that point, we were, like, let's get married or move on. I liked him, so we did. But things got boring eventually, and marriage made it worse, you know?"

"Yes, married men make me rich," said Hasan.

"I bet. Anyway, we wanted to stay together, so we tried other things: bondage, which I liked but he didn't, and playing with others."

"Open marriage?"

"Yes. It was fun but a lot of work."

"Why?"

"Finding the right person was always tricky. So, he got tired and let me play on my own."

"Lucky. The men I meet," said Hasan and struggled for the English word. "*Kurban*. Sacrifice, would sacrifice their kids to do that."

"I sure would, too. After a while, I realized prostitutes were the easiest way. They'd actually show up, without all the work in a fucking app, the drama, and the expectations and shit. And you pros will do almost anything for money. Unlike the pansies who would back out when I told them I like dominating." He flexed his left bicep and squeezed it.

Hasan took a moment to process what he'd heard. He realized that when Adam called him *pro* in the hotel, he did mean *prostitute*. Deflated, he said, "I understand. Every man need us for their escape."

"Yeah, the irony of preaching monogamy yet fucking prostitutes. And I lost Mark because of it."

"Why?"

"Well, my last pro in DC was a wild son of a bitch. He would do anything on a dare. We got shitfaced one night, and he started running through ideas. His first idea was to streak by the White House naked. His second idea was to have sex in the National Mall."

"Shopping?"

"No, no, it's a giant park surrounded by government buildings, national monuments, and a reflecting pool in the middle."

"Oh, okay," said Hasan.

"The idea of it was exciting, and you could maybe get away with a hand job there, but I said no to that. I was drunk, not fucking stupid. We settled on smoking pot, still illegal but more discreet. We were pulled aside by one of the feds. He probably wouldn't even have arrested us, if my trick hadn't tweaked and tried to run away—turns out he already had an arrest warrant for robbery and assault—so we both got hauled in. This was the last straw for Mark, who bailed me out, and he left me soon after because he said he didn't want to deal with my bullshit anymore. That was the end of us."

"Bad boy," said Hasan, even if he didn't understand everything. Every man had a story, and his job was to listen. The wind picked up in the afternoon heat, and Hasan saw a ripe apple hit the ground nearby in the orchard.

Adam rattled on, getting worked up as he emptied his plastic cup. He wiped his thin *ayran* moustache before he dug into his baklava and said, "But you know what, despite all that happened, I remember feeling relief, liberated at the end. I mean, yes, gay rights have become marriage rights—I believe in the right to marry in principle—but it's the end of gay culture as we know it. Soon, we'll act like the breeders, cleaning after children, arranging play dates, all that shit, until they grow up and leave us to die. The worst part is, behind the facade, all the guys cheat on one another and ditch the loves of their lives as soon as they find the next best guy. It is a fucking charade, and we can't call it what it is. Now you know."

"And this the goal for cute boys at the network?" said Hasan. "Why not tell?"

"You think that's what they want to hear? Plus, I don't think gay marriage will happen here. It's taking almost two generations in the States, and look at the mess we've made. Turkey's basically third-world, and its shit is messier."

Hasan watched Adam squeeze the plastic *ayran* cup out of shape. He reminded himself again that he was working, and this guy was paying him to escape reality, so he put his hand under the table and rubbed Adam's thigh and said, "It's okay. Let's enjoy."

Hasan withdrew his hand as the tour guide approached their table and announced that they were leaving in ten minutes. Adam said he needed to stop by the restroom, and Hasan told him he'd meet him in the bus. Alone at the table with Adam's empty tray and his still half full, with his baklava untouched, he gazed at the rows of fruit trees that seemed to stretch to infinity under the scorching sun. He wondered if Adam believed in anything or anyone. How could he be so liberated and yet so unhappy? His cynicism at the expense of the young, hopeful activists who hung on his every word depressed Hasan. The naiveté of his wish at the Water of Mary fountain in Ephesus enveloped him like the heat that infiltrated his clothes and made his skin damp and sticky.

Their last stop was a prearranged visit to a roadside leather clothing factory next to vast, harvested wheat fields dotted with bales of hay. Another empty van belonging to a different tour company sat in the parking lot adjacent to a small concrete warehouse that had a corrugated metal roof. They were led into a small retail area in the front. A shopkeeper greeted them, and they saw another group of a dozen or so tourists browsing the racks. Beyond the double doors with small windows at the back of the room, they could see factory workers hunched over and cutting and sewing processed leather at their workstations. The cashier announced in English that the show would start in five minutes and that they would have time to shop afterward.

"A show? What the hell?" said Adam.

"A fashion show? Wait and see," said Hasan.

Soon, they were ushered into another, larger room with bare walls and a *T*-shaped catwalk in the middle. Four rows of folding chairs that together could probably seat sixty people spanned the width of the room and faced the top of the *T*. As soon as they were seated, the lights went off and club music started blasting through the speakers on each side of the room, accompanied by strobe lights that moved to the music. Hasan and Adam gave each other is-this-really-happening looks.

Several spotlights flashed onto the catwalk, and three models, a man and two women probably in their twenties, walked out from behind a curtain. Olive-skinned, the guy appeared Turkish; he wore sunglasses with a black leather jacket and blue jeans. Slender and tall in stilettos, the women didn't seem Turkish; both had lily-white skin, crimson lips, and straight, bleached blond hair down to their calves. One wore red leather dungarees and the other a low-cut blue top and black leather shorts. Hasan was mesmerized, as if he were watching a train wreck.

They strutted down the catwalk as they eyed the audience like cheetahs stalking gazelles on the savannah. When they reached the end of the runway, the man nodded to the music as the women rolled their heads, whipping their hair and contorting their lanky torsos to the beat. Their hair furled and unfurled in the air as it reflected the spotlights. Hasan caught a glimpse of a few wisps of black hair under the blond mane of one of the women. After about thirty seconds, the women positioned themselves on each side of the male model and rested their heads on his shoulders as he lowered his glasses and cast a sleazy look at the audience.

They performed several similar routines, taking a minute or two between segments to change clothes behind a curtain. Each time they did it, the dreamlike absurdity of the show alternated with its incongruous reality in the roadside warehouse. At the end of the show, the deafening music finally stopped, and the strobe lights and spotlights went off, leaving them in complete darkness for a few seconds before rows of fluorescent lights flickered on. The catwalk was empty, and it seemed like the models just disappeared into thin air. The twenty-minute show felt like a hallucination during a drug trip.

They were immediately herded back to the retail section. Hasan needed some fresh air, so they agreed to meet outside after Adam browsed the racks. As Hasan walked out into the smoldering Aegean afternoon heat radiating from the asphalt lot, he smelled cigarette smoke and saw the trio of models to his left on the shadier side of the building. They saw him, too, but didn't look at him for more than a second.

Hasan wondered if the women were Rus immigrants who left communist poverty in search of dreams in a new land and instead found themselves caught in this corner of the Aegean countryside pandering over and over to tourists from around the world. With one arm akimbo, they each sucked on the filters of their cigarettes and squinted their eyes from the smoke, revealing a certain defiance and hardness despite their seeming youth.

Hasan recognized that look; it occurred to him that they might moonlight as sex workers. He trusted his hunch—it took one to know one. He was pretty sure modeling wasn't their sole occupation, even if they might have wanted it to be. He thought back to their fifteen minutes of fame on the runway, god knows how many times a day, before they probably left at the end of the day for the Kordon, the famous seaside promenade of downtown Izmir, where outdoor bars were hotbeds of nightly entertainment in the summer. They'd be ogled and whistled at by men and eventually bedded by one or more who, like most Turkish men, had insatiable lust for blondes, real or fake, and would never respect them.

His thoughts were interrupted when Adam sauntered out with two large shopping bags. Unlike the models, the daylight enhanced his middle-aged good looks. As he walked by the models, they eyeballed Adam and glanced at Hasan, whispered something to each other, and giggled. They seemed to recognize the parts Hasan and Adam played today. When he reached Hasan, Adam gestured back at the models with his head and said, "What the fuck was that show? Models my ass. More like whores. Fucking losers."

Hasan looked at them for a few seconds and sighed. "Yes, trash," he said.

As they turned to walk toward the van, Hasan looked back. One of the women met his gaze. He smiled at her, and she waved. He quickly raised his hand in response and turned back around.

They were the first to board the van for the trip back to Izmir. Hasan asked Adam, "Find a Turkish leather toy you like?"

Adam played along. "I got a whip."

"Oof, it will hurt," said Hasan as he watched the rest of their party walk over in twos and threes and get on board. Another van arrived with a fresh batch of tourists, and the models stamped on their cigarette butts and ducked inside.

As the bus idled, Hasan said, "Fun day. *Teşekkürler.*"

"Thank you for the company," said Adam and squeezed Hasan's thigh. He slid down in his seat a little and seemed sleepy.

As Adam made himself comfortable for a nap, Hasan replayed their time together: their fiery night, the passionate morning, his wish at Meryem Ana Evi, Adam's bitter words at the restaurant, and the show just now. "I'll tell my wish," he said.

Adam half-opened his eyes.

"I wanted to know you more," said Hasan.

"You could've just asked me," said Adam and added, "There's no more to know than I already told you." He closed his eyes.

Outside the window, the Aegean countryside slowly gave way to the valleys and hillsides of Izmir increasingly overgrown with closely built apartment buildings. Hasan wished to go back to the leather factory someday with gregarious Mehmet, who would speak with the models. He wanted him to see the show and confirm their real story.

As Adam slept, he texted Mehmet, *"Efes'teydik bugün, şimdi yol-dayım"*—we visited Ephesus, and I'm on my way to you.

PRIDE

Cenk checked his Rolex as he waited for his car. It was past 11:00 p.m. on Saturday, June 27, 2015. The glass over the black dial with silver numbers reflected the multicolored lights from the towering Boğaziçi Bridge, which was less than two hundred meters away and dominated the skyline. The changing lights zigzagged like the pattern on a backgammon board.

He had just exited Reina, a posh, sprawling entertainment venue in Istanbul's seaside neighborhood of Ortaköy. Reina's interior looked like a cruise deck, with glittering views of the Bosphorus and the suspension bridge; it had chic dining rooms on the periphery and a nightclub area in the middle with a bar and a dance floor under a massive outdoor chandelier. A trendy spot for jetsetters and global celebrities like Paris Hilton, Salma Hayek, and Mike Tyson, Reina had a strict "smart dress" policy, with long lines for those who weren't on the VIP list.

Cenk left behind Tuncay, a longtime friend since kindergarten; Alper, a friend from college; and their fiancées, Zuhal and Beyza, at Reina. The couples fancied themselves matchmakers, so they brought Zeynep, a brunette. She had an alluring smile and wore a peach satin wraparound dress with a plunging neckline. They exchanged numbers, even if he wasn't sure he was going to call her. His mother would consider her a perfect catch, but he wasn't ready to be tied down. He couldn't pursue another woman in front of them, either, so he had to seek other pastures for his pleasure tonight.

He tipped the handsome young valet, who brought his new silver BMW convertible, and set out for Taksim. He had received his bachelor's degree in construction engineering from Istanbul Technical University two weeks ago, and the car was his parents' graduation gift. As Nazlı *Hanım*, his mother, suggested, he was taking the summer off before starting work at his family's construction company. He loosened his tie and inhaled the new-car smell of the creamy leather interior of the M6; its 560hp engine was a perfect metaphor for the possibilities of a long, adventurous summer.

He parked in a garage near Taksim Square on top of a hill that overlooked the Boğaziçi Strait. He took off his tie and jacket and placed them in the passenger seat, and unbuttoned his dress shirt down to his sternum. He didn't want to park such an expensive car in what he knew to be a congested, seedy area, so he hailed a cab for the short ride to Tek Yön, One Way. He had recently heard about this nightclub from Osman, a friend in his early forties whom he met through Hornet. Osman was married, but Cenk and he got together to let off steam when his wife was out of town visiting his in-laws. Osman said that Tek Yön was the place to go for plenty of *kuir* fish.

The cab dropped him off in front of a nondescript building on one of the back streets of the Beyoğlu entertainment district. Were it not for the faint sound of muffled music and a few men who smoked near the entrance and eyeballed him, he wouldn't have been able to tell there was a club in the basement of the old building.

The bouncer checked his ID and patted him down. He walked down a steep flight of exposed concrete stairs. The club was low-lit and smelled of cheap beer. He grabbed an Efes at the bar and took in the ambience as his eyes adjusted to the darkness. Empty vinyl booths, some with cracks that revealed their spongy padding, surrounded the dance floor. Eight or nine college-aged men danced to Tarkan's "*Acımayacak*," "It Won't Hurt," blaring from the speakers.

A ring of mostly older, middle-aged men stood on the sidelines and watched them. Unlike Reina's suave, manicured patrons in fashionable clothes, these men wore jeans and T-shirts, and their beards, moustaches, and *esmer*, weathered skin projected a tough, hardworking masculinity. He remembered what Osman said about Tek Yön's clientele profile: *inşaat işçileri*, construction workers. This description made Cenk think of "rough trade," his favorite category of gay porn, with muscular and hairy yet trimmed American men who acted as plumbers, carpenters, or lumberjacks—and it was all the better if they happened to be more mature.

After he finished his beer, his third drink of the night, Cenk stepped onto the dance floor, expecting one of the men to approach. A few tried their luck, but Cenk wasn't interested.

Soon, a salt-and-pepper-haired, bearded man, who seemed around forty, approached and began dancing with him. He wore a soccer jersey over jeans that showed off his slim yet muscular build.

After they locked eyes, he yelled his name into his ear, "I'm Gökhan." Cenk shouted his own name back.

They bumped heads as they tried to have a conversation. The music was too loud, so they continued dancing. Their bodies became attuned to one another as the heat rose around them.

When Gökhan finally grabbed Cenk and kissed him, Cenk felt as if the air and sound had been sucked out of the club.

After the kiss, Gökhan raised his thick eyebrows as he smiled, gesturing with his thumb toward the exit like a hitchhiker.

Cenk nodded. His blood coursed through his veins like pure caffeine.

As they exited the club, Gökhan said, "Come to my place. I live nearby, in Tarlabaşı."

"*Tamam*," said Cenk. He felt tingly all over.

They crossed the Tarlabaşı Bulvarı, which wound down the hill from Taksim Square toward Haliç, the Golden Horn. Gökhan pointed down the boulevard and said, "I work at the Euro Plaza Hotel that way."

"Interesting," said Cenk. "How did you get into that?"

"By necessity," said Gökhan. "Not my first choice after a master's in art history."

"Sorry," said Cenk. "I hope you're able to eventually use your degree."

"That's the problem. I didn't want to teach, and jobs at museums were hard to come by, so I went into tourism," said Gökhan.

"Smart," said Cenk.

"Well, they made me start at the lowest level, as a bellboy, and it's taken me a decade to make it to the front desk." Gökhan sighed. "What about you?"

"I'm a construction engineer, just graduated from ITU," said Cenk. "I'm taking the summer off before I start working for my family's company."

"*Güzel, tebrikler,*" said Gökhan. "I wish I could take some time off. I recently enrolled in a tour guide certification program, and that keeps me busy."

In Cenk's memories of being driven through Taksim as a child, this neighborhood had dilapidated buildings with freshly laundered clothes swinging like flags on lines strung between them. He remembered seeing barefoot kids playing on the streets. Now, newly constructed condominiums and a shopping mall dominated the area. Cenk wondered if his family's company had a hand in the change.

When they veered north off the main boulevard, new quickly gave way to old as they traveled downhill. Three-to-four-floor apartment buildings stood shoulder to shoulder and formed long rows on both sides of the narrow, winding streets. The cement exteriors wore faded reds, grays, yellows, and greens of old frayed clothes. Bay windows protruded like noses from the upper floors, shrinking the night sky.

On the northern edge of the neighborhood near the bottom of the hill, they entered one of the old buildings and proceeded down a marble staircase to an apartment in the basement. There was a slightly musty scent. When Gökhan unlocked the door and welcomed him inside, Cenk's first thought was that the studio apartment was smaller than their garage in Bebek. The room had a futon across from a TV set, and there were two small rectangular windows on top of the wall that faced away from the hill. To the left of the entrance was a kitchenette with a stove, sink, and small counter space over a cabinet and minifridge.

"*Hoş geldin,*" said Gökhan.

"*Hoş bulduk,*" said Cenk. "Could you direct me to the bathroom, *lütfen?*" As he and his friends liked saying, beer was indeed not owned but rented.

Gökhan extended his hand with a flourish toward the apartment's only door other than the entrance, across from the kitchenette. "This way, *efendim*. Give me a ring if you get lost on the way back."

"I don't even have your number. You'll have to send a search party."

Cenk closed the bathroom door. The toilet was wedged between the shower cabin and the sink. Because he was aroused, it took him longer than usual to pee. He next went through his pre-hookup checklist: wash face, check teeth, rinse mouth, comb hair, and smell armpits—they were okay; he always kept his pits trimmed and overapplied deodorant. He smoothed his eyebrows with his wet middle fingers before he dried his hands and returned to Gökhan's living room-kitchen-bedroom.

Gökhan stood up when Cenk came out of the bathroom and said, "My turn. Make yourself comfortable."

Cenk paced around the room. On the wall above the TV, wooden-handled signs with slogans were mounted around a large rainbow flag:

Yürüyoruz! "We are marching!"

Velev ki ibneyiz. "So what if we are fags?"

Trans candır. "Trans is a dear life."

Ahlaksızız. "We are immoral."

Ahlakınız batsın! "Down with your morality!"

Gökhan came out of the bathroom in his white undershirt that highlighted his olive skin and gray-streaked hair. "Want an Efes?"

"*Evet, teşekkürler,*" said Cenk.

Gökhan grabbed two beers from his minifridge and passed one to Cenk. He gestured with his beer bottle at the rainbow paraphernalia on the wall and asked, "Have you ever marched in Onur Yürüyüşü?"

"Isn't it tomorrow?" said Cenk.

"Yes," said Gökhan.

"I went once like five years ago, in high school," said Cenk and took a big sip of his beer. "I'm bisexual. You?"

"Ah, one of those," said Gökhan and smiled. "I'm *gey.*"

"Your wall says it all. *Şerefe,*" said Cenk.

"*Şerefe,*" repeated Gökhan.

They clinked bottles and drank. Gökhan had a warm smile with cute dimples. Cenk leaned toward Gökhan and stroked his beard. When they kissed, he tasted the beer in Gökhan's mouth. The long kisses felt like finally letting go after holding his breath for a while.

They watched each other undress. Gökhan wore white briefs and had a hairy chest and legs; on his left shoulder was a tattoo of a peace sign in rainbow colors, with *Savaşma Seviş,* "Make Love, Not War," encircling it. Cenk's boxers were printed with divebombing propeller planes. His trimmed red chest hair showed off his pecs.

"I like your boxers," said Gökhan.

"Thanks," said Cenk. "I like your tattoo."

"My motto," said Gökhan.

Cenk touched the tattoo with his index finger and said, "I'm all for that." He pulled down his boxers.

Gökhan gulped down the rest of his beer. He put the empty bottle aside, stood up, and pulled the futon open. As he took off his briefs, he asked Cenk, "Are you *aktif* or *pasif*?"

"*Aktif*," said Cenk, "You?"

"I'm *aktif*, too," said Gökhan.

Cenk expected this response. As his fuck buddy Osman jokingly put it, they all, especially older men, claimed to be *aktif* to not tarnish their manhood and then turned their backs in bed. But in this case, he hoped that it was true. With women, Cenk was *aktif* as the man; with men, he liked the option to be the center of attention, the object of desire. So he said, "I actually go with the vibe I get from a person." He didn't usually share this truth unless the feeling was right.

"What's my vibe?" said Gökhan.

Cenk eyeballed him head to toe and said, "Let's see how *aktif* you are."

"I'll show you," said Gökhan and tackled Cenk onto the futon.

Gökhan was close enough to Cenk's rough-trade fantasy in his drunken state. But Gökhan turned out to be more than that. His touch alternated between gentleness and forcefulness toward the kind of climax Cenk's pulsing, yearning body hadn't had for a while.

After they finished, they laid on the bed. Cenk savored the moment, until Gökhan said, "I hope you don't mind me asking: Do you think bisexuality is a phase?"

"In high school, we all experimented," said Cenk. He reached out for his clothes and got up to dress. Gay men always wanted to chat about this stuff. The others wanted you to leave as soon as possible, with no such small talk, to his relief.

"Do you still see them? Are they *heteroseksüel* now?" said Gökhan as he grabbed his briefs and put them on.

"Pretty much," said Cenk.

"Is that what you'll do?"

"I don't know. If I fall in love with a woman, no problem. If I fall in love with a man . . . I'll cross that bridge when it comes."

"What about your parents, do they know?" asked Gökhan.

"My mother does, wants me to hide it," said Cenk.

"That's better than how my parents reacted," said Gökhan. "I didn't come out. My mother found *LeGeBeTe* brochures in my backpack—I had just started volunteering for Lambda Istanbul—and told my father. He confronted me, as she cried quietly. He didn't even let me speak, told me that a man like him can't have an *eşcinsel* son—he was an officer in the army—that it's a sin. They've been hoping and expecting me to change ever since, but *gey* is what I am."

"I'm sorry," said Cenk.

"About me being *gey* or my parents?" said Gökhan.

"Your parents, of course," said Cenk. "I prefer you *gey.*"

"You should come to Lambda Istanbul," said Gökhan, "Where I still volunteer. That organization is why I live here now."

"Where did you live before?"

"Bağcılar."

"I've never been," said Cenk, "Is that where you're from?"

"No, I'm from Çorlu," said Gökhan. "Bağcılar is midway between my parents' and Mimar Sinan, where I was doing my master's at the time, but I don't visit them as often anymore. Anyway, you can meet other *LeGeBeTe'ler* at Lambda Istanbul."

"I could do that," said Cenk.

"You probably have plans," said Gökhan as he stood up, "but would you like to come to the march tomorrow? There is a party afterward."

"Do you think it's going to happen? I heard the governor banned it."

"That won't stop us, we'll try anyway," said Gökhan.

Cenk hesitated for a moment. He couldn't quite bring himself to say no to Gökhan's expectant face, so he said, "Text me the specifics."

"*Tamam,*" said Gökhan.

They exchanged numbers and had one last kiss before Cenk left. He hailed a cab back to the garage. As he drove his BMW home, he debated whether he should accept Gökhan's invitation and what he'd text back if he didn't.

When Nazlı *Hanım* woke up in the morning, her first thought was the same as her last right after she'd heard Cenk come home past midnight: that she wanted a report about why he returned home so late. She could've asked him then, but she didn't want an argument before sleep.

Awaiting his appearance any moment yet hiding her impatience, she side-eyed the sliding glass door to the deck of their estate in the wooded hillside, where she was having breakfast facing the Bosphorus as Sevda, their live-in maid, waited on her. Nazlı *Hanım* wore black Jackie O sunglasses from Vint & York; big, square lenses covered most of the upper half of her face. Her red hair, henna-dyed to hide a few gray and white strands, was sprayed into a helmet with a tight bun at the back. She eyeballed Sevda's back as Sevda walked inside, like she didn't want to let her out of sight.

Nazlı *Hanım*'s name meant "reluctant or coy" in Turkish, and that was what many who didn't know better thought about her back when she lived with her parents in Çorlu. Looking back, Nazlı *Hanım* would've characterized herself as "resistant," because life as a young *lezbiyen* in 1980s Çorlu was out of her control. Resistance, including her onetime attempt at her own life, bought her some freedom from parental constraints at twenty-one, allowing her to drive, work, and delay marriage. The following year, in 1990, she left her parents' home for Istanbul to study typing and stenography while staying with relatives.

Twenty-five years later, at forty-seven, she was fully in control now; friends and family affectionately called her *hükümet gibi kadın*, a woman like a government, and sought her counsel about matters of importance. It took many years to develop that reputation. She met Cevdet *Bey*, Cenk's father, in 1993 when she was hired as a secretary at his company. He was her first and only boss who didn't try to grope her in the office. She was twenty-five and he was forty-five. He fell in love with her, and she liked him—and all of the closeted lesbians she knew ended up marrying a man as a safety net anyway—so they got married the same year, and she was pregnant with Cenk soon after.

Nazlı *Hanım*'s mother-in-law and three sisters-in-law disapproved of the marriage, and they belittled her for her family's humble means and treated her like an ingénue in a melodrama. Cevdet *Bey* was pained to watch the disparagement she endured in those early years, so he treated her like an equal and encouraged her to study business administration through Açıköğretim, a video-based education program from Anadolu Üniversitesi. He taught her everything about the family business, including its finances. As he aged and his health declined, Nazlı *Hanım* gradually took the reins of the family and their business. She now embraced her role as the matriarch, leading their company expertly through the people she handpicked to work for her.

Nazlı *Hanım* let Cenk know that she never took her position for granted, as she told him many times about the humiliations she had suffered at the hands of his grandmother and aunts, including being called a *lezbiyen* as an insult when she started attending company meetings and wore a pantsuit. She wasn't vengeful toward those who had treated her badly, but maintaining a tough exterior, which had been essential to her survival, became second nature to her. She didn't tell Cenk that their epithet for her was correct.

Nazlı *Hanım*'s favorite saying was, "*Nasıl varırsan, o şekilde görülürsün*"—the way you arrive is the way people see you, so she was pleased to watch Cenk check his reflection on the floor-to-ceiling mirror in the living room that opened to the deck. He had red hair like hers and leaned in toward the mirror to make sure that he hadn't missed any sleep in his eyes, as she used to have him do when he was a child. He also checked the sides of his neck—for a "bite of love"? Nazlı *Hanım* predicted that he was with someone last night, and couldn't wait to find out.

She watched Cenk walk through their spacious living room. Large leaves of *deve tabanı* fanned upward at two corners of the room. An enormous handwoven silk carpet anchored the room at its center. A sofa and armchairs with gold brocade were placed around a marble coffee table, which had a beautiful centerpiece of multicolored roses. Their gardener replenished the centerpiece every other morning. A long ottoman stood in front of the floor-to-ceiling windows that overlooked the woods and the strait in the distance. Cenk liked teasing her that viewed in the daylight, the all-glass facade reminded him of a crystal doorknob of an all-marble restroom he saw at the Topkapı Sarayı, the sprawling Ottoman palace-turned-museum in the old city. As he crossed the room, he looked up at their framed oil portrait of Mustafa Kemal Atatürk, the founding father of the Republic, whose blue eyes watched all of them. She often wondered what Atatürk, the staunch secularist, would say about the country's increasingly Islamist direction. Cenk slid open the door to the deck and walked out.

"Nazlı *Hanım*, you look beautiful as usual," said Cenk and hugged her.

She kissed his cheek without taking her sunglasses off.

"*Merhaba paşam*, your excellency has finally honored us with his presence," she said. "I heard you get in very late last night. Where were you?"

"I was with a friend after Reina," said Cenk.

"A girlfriend?"

"No, it was Gökhan, a friend I met yesterday." He didn't know why he mentioned his name. He certainly wouldn't be going into detail about how they met.

"What does Gökhan do?" said Nazlı *Hanım*. The name reminded her of the neighbor's son from back in her hometown of Çorlu, but she dismissed the thought, as he couldn't possibly be the same person.

"He's a receptionist at a hotel. He has a master's degree in art history but works in the tourism industry."

"I see," she said. "You're planning to see him again?"

"Yes."

She took off her sunglasses and said, "You are not doing as we agreed then."

"*Anne*—"

"Don't argue with me. Have you forgotten our agreement?"

"How could I? You remind me every time," said Cenk.

Their maid, Sevda, stepped onto the deck. Nazlı *Hanım* looked into the distance toward the Boğaziçi Bridge, suspended like a diamond choker across the strait. Sevda said hello, served Cenk's tea, and left.

Cenk sat up in his chair, leaned forward, and said, "I guess you're too afraid to speak freely around your maid?"

"I am not afraid of Sevda or anyone else, but don't think for one second there isn't a price for being in control. I'll fire her on the spot and make sure she won't get a job in this town if she squeaks a word. But you have a responsibility here, too."

Nazlı *Hanım* not only trusted Sevda but also loved her. Sevda had come recommended from another wealthy family fifteen years ago, and they'd been lovers for a decade now. With ailing health in his late sixties, her husband Cevdet *Bey* let Nazlı *Hanım* be, and Sevda's being a live-in maid facilitated their romance behind closed doors; unbeknownst to anyone, including Cenk and his father, they had become life companions, yet this was a secret they both knew they had to guard with their lives.

"*Anne*, I haven't violated our agreement."

"Why are you associating with Gökhan then? His family must be nothing like us."

"*Anne*—"

"Remember you promised me not to mix with *travestiler* and *lümpen* gays? You know they'll take advantage of you, right?"

Nazlı *Hanım* had felt like she was shot in the forehead when he told her at sixteen that he was *biseksüel*. Being who she was, she first wondered how she missed the signs. Her beloved son was nothing like the gay men she had recently encountered: the flashy yet ambiguous singers on television, the fashionable single men she knew from Istanbul's jet set, or their retired director of finance, a bookish perpetual bachelor who had a longtime male friend who had accompanied him to every social function and whom he introduced as his "business associate." Of course, everyone knew or suspected who was what, and whispers straggled through the grapevine, but no one dared to state the obvious publicly, unless they wanted to destroy lives by ruining one's reputation.

She thought bisexuality was the gateway to homosexuality, so she refused to speak to Cenk about the subject for several days as she pondered the possibilities. When they finally spoke, she declared, "We can manage this. At least you're not *gey.*" But she feared that he would still get blackmailed, so she made him promise that he'd marry a woman and limit his affairs with men to those who had as much to lose as Cenk did if the affair came out.

Cenk sighed. "I know what I promised, but—"

"You don't know what you're getting yourself into if you don't listen to me. You're our only son." She spread her arms to signal their surroundings and said, "All of this will be yours one day, but do you think religious bureaucrats will work with an *ibne?* Our company does a lot of work for the government."

Cenk stood up. "You don't know what you're saying, and you don't know what you're asking me."

"I know what's at stake. Don't treat me like I'm one of those naïve girls you sleep with between your boyfriends."

Cenk grimaced. "I'm seeing him again today," he said before he turned around and walked away.

As he exited, Nazlı *Hanım* said, "Remember, once people see you a certain way, there is no going back."

Cenk and Gökhan met early in the afternoon in front of the Marmara Hotel on Taksim Square, which was a short walk from the beginning of the Pride March route on the pedestrian-only Istiklal Street, Istanbul's most famous thoroughfare, in Beyoğlu. Formerly Pera, this western-ized, historically European neighborhood had seen the rise and fall of the non-Muslim minorities from the Ottoman Empire to the Republic of Turkey. They joined several hundred marchers there. The crowd pulsed with rainbow colors, and signs held high showed slogans like *LGBTİ hakları insan haklarıdır*—"LGBTI rights are human rights"—and *Lezbiyenler vardır*—"Lesbians exist." Some were dressed in flamboyant costumes and makeup; a drag queen with a beard and sequined dress towered above others in the middle of the crowd.

"Why aren't we moving?" said Cenk.

Gökhan craned his neck. "I see policemen in riot gear blocking the route. This will turn into Gezi again. Let's move back."

It was the two-year anniversary of the Gezi Park protests, which were held on the other side of the square in summer 2013. Cenk had seen on television the skirmishes between teargassed protestors and the masked police.

They retreated a couple of hundred meters back to Taksim Square. When the marchers ahead refused to leave, the police shot tear gas canisters at the crowd. Some started yelling and booing. Others covered their faces and coughed as they staggered away. When a few wearing gas masks or covering their mouths and noses with kerchiefs or ban-danas continued protesting, they were sprayed with high-power water jets from the police's Toplumsal Olaylara Müdahale Aracı, Vehicles to Intervene in Societal Events.

Cenk's eyes began to water, and he felt a tickle in his throat. He turned to Gökhan and asked, "What should we do? I don't want to get arrested."

"We won't get arrested, but I don't want you to inhale tear gas or get injured," said Gökhan. "Let's try to take another route to Tünel." He put his arm around Cenk's shoulder, and they ducked into a side street.

The march always ended at Tünel, the historic subway funicular line built in the 1870s at the end of Istiklal Street. In the small square in front of the station, the activists would hold a press briefing and read the collective declaration about LGBT rights endorsed by various advocacy organizations. Cenk and Gökhan walked south down the hill and away from the square to try to circumvent the cordoned areas. But they kept encountering police barricades, so after several attempts, they gave up and decided to see if they could get to the afterparty.

The club Mekan was on the fourth floor of an old building off the opposite side of Istiklal Street, so they had to walk another half hour to get back up to and around Taksim Square. The area had quieted down as people dispersed, but there still was a heavy police presence.

Cenk and Gökhan entered the building, which had no elevator. Before they climbed four flights of eroded white marble stairs, Cenk looked up at the dark polished mahogany that snaked along the top of the ironwork railing all the way to the skylight.

The music got louder as they climbed the stairs. When they reached the top floor, a bouncer opened the door, and the club's lights, pink like cotton candy, washed over them. The dance floor was mostly empty. There were a few people standing at the bar and around the DJ's station. Some lounged at the high-top tables by the walls. The realization that the party was still on was a relief to Cenk, a return to normalcy amid chaos.

"I'll get us drinks. Grab a table," said Gökhan and walked over to the bar area.

Five minutes later, Gökhan returned from the bar with a group of his friends in tow. Cenk listened as they discussed over drinks the banning of the march for the first time. It had been allowed to take place for the previous twelve years, through 2014.

"They say security risk and public sensitivities, but I think they're finally getting back at us for Gezi," said Ayşe, a lesbian activist and web designer who was there with her girlfriend Nilgün, an elementary school teacher. They seemed so in love, unable to keep their hands off each other.

"Same-sex marriage gets legalized in America, and this's what we get," said Nilgün.

"That, and they're emboldened by the new homeland security law. We can be arrested and held for up to forty-eight hours without reason," said Ekrem, a chubby guy with blue highlights who eyeballed the men on the dance floor, which was beginning to fill up. Cenk was surprised that he was even listening.

Gökhan added, "And the fact that the march was scheduled during Ramadan."

Ekrem said, "Well, yes, but what about Ramadan last year? We marched as planned, didn't we?" He didn't wait for a response. He put his empty glass on the side table and strode into the dancing crowd.

"What about that nationalist youth group that threatened on Facebook and Twitter to disrupt the march?" asked Nilgün as she leaned into Ayşe.

"Instead of doing something about it, the governor's office pounced on that as a perfect excuse to ban the march," said Gökhan.

A passing drag queen leaned in and said, "Did someone die?"

Cenk laughed while the others stared at her.

Gökhan said, "Well, not today, but don't you remember Berkin Elvan last year?"

"Of course, I remember, *canım*. May the kid rest in heaven," said the drag queen and sighed. "I feel terrible, too, and my heels and tuck are killing me. But if we cannot stand up to them on the street, we get back at them by partying harder, right? Let's go, *şekerler*." She beckoned them toward the dance floor, looking like their excessively made-up fairy godmother who wanted to protect them from the ash of the world.

Cenk was beginning to feel depressed as he listened to Gökhan and others. He had come to drink and dance. He took the drag queen's cue and grabbed Gökhan by the hand and pulled him to the dance floor. Dancing to pop music remixed with electronic beats, they quickly forgot about the world outside.

As the sun set, the DJ transitioned to slower music. Cenk and Gökhan held each other and kissed.

When Chinawoman's "Kiss in Taksim Square," about the Gezi Park protests, came on, everyone went wild and sang in unison:

One idiot is all that it takes

. . .

One idiot ruins one thousand fates

Just as the song ended, Cenk heard screams from the balcony of the fourth-floor club, where people smoked, and the music suddenly stopped. A plume of gas billowed in from the balcony. People ran inside, and Cenk's throat and eyes felt like they were on fire. Gökhan told him to cover his nose and mouth. Cenk ran across the room and grabbed a rainbow flag hanging from the bar counter and pressed it to his face. It was like putting your face against a screen door; the cheap synthetic fabric of the flag felt like rough plastic. Everyone around him was coughing violently and gasping for air.

Covered up to his eyes with the flag, like a bandit in a Western, he watched a woman pass out as others stepped over her and ran to the stairs. A few people stopped and tended to her. One of them grabbed a bottle of water from the bar and sprinkled her face trying to revive her. Cenk breathed with difficulty, and his temples throbbed. He coughed a few times as his eyes watered, tears rolling down his cheeks like glass beads. He rubbed his eyes with his shirtsleeve as he looked toward the stairs. The exit was clogged with people. He looked around in panic, scanning the club's walls for an emergency exit. There was none. He closed his eyes and said Ayetel Kürsi, a prayer for protection his mother taught him when he was a child.

When he opened his eyes, Gökhan was nowhere to be seen. Cenk panicked and texted him immediately. *Nerdesin??* No response. He walked around in the emptying club, asking people about him. No one knew where he was. He checked the restrooms. Did he leave without telling him?

Cenk came back to the dance floor. The club was almost empty now, and the staircase was clear. He stood under the disco ball that spun in an eerie silence broken by sporadic coughs. Mini squares of lights reflected off the disco ball's mirrors circulated on the walls as if they were closing in on him. As he stood transfixed, he felt a tap on the back and spun around, letting go off the flag, and without realizing, he stepped on it.

"What the hell are you waiting for?" yelled Gökhan, squinting and grimacing because of the remnants of tear gas in the room.

"I've been looking for you all over this place! You take me here and leave me?" said Cenk.

"I went downstairs thinking you were behind me. I turned around on the street and you were nowhere to be found. Are you okay?"

"Yes," said Cenk and rubbed his eyes.

Gökhan extended his hand and said, "Let's go." Cenk grabbed it and followed him down the stairs.

On their way out, they let their hands go when they saw a group of police officers patrolling the street. Cenk wondered if they were the ones who had shot the gas canister onto the club's balcony. They looked his age or even younger, including one who was very handsome in his uniform. He wondered how such a beautiful creature could do such an evil thing.

They kept walking until they reached a quiet street. Gökhan put his palms on his knees and coughed away the remnants of tear gas in his system. Cenk leaned back against the cool stone wall of a building.

He felt the hard surface of the block stone against his hands, back, and scalp as he looked up to the full moon. He inhaled the fresh air. His breathing was still ragged, and his eyes continued watering, but the feeling of panic slowly subsided.

There was a *büfe* across the street. They bought a couple of bottled waters and drank and washed their faces on the cobbled street.

Cenk checked his phone and saw a message from his mother: "Are you staying out tonight?" He put his phone in his pocket and turned to Gökhan. "It's my mother. I'd better go."

"I cannot believe they'd do this after all they did to prevent the march," said Gökhan. "They don't want us to do anything *LeGeBeTe*."

"Or to be one," said Cenk. "Why are you surprised?"

"*Özür dilerim*," said Gökhan, "It's my fault. I shouldn't have brought you here."

"I brought this on myself," said Cenk.

"What do you mean?"

"It doesn't matter. I should go."

"Am I going to see you again?" said Gökhan.

"Yeah, sure. Text me," said Cenk.

They had a quick hug. Cenk walked away without another word and hailed a cab to the parking garage.

Once in his car, Cenk texted his mother that he'd be home soon. He took the coastal road along the Bosphorus to Bebek. He passed by the nineteenth-century Dolmabahçe Sarayı in Beşiktaş, the iconic Ortaköy Mosque by the Bosphorus Bridge, and old *yali* mansions in Arnavutköy along the water before Bebek. *Yakamoz*, the moonglade, journeyed with him on the water as he drove and contemplated whether he'd tell his mother what had just happened, and if he'd see Gökhan again.

Cenk turned onto the road that led to his family's estate on the hillside overlooking the tranquil Bebek coast. When he arrived at the gate, he idled his car, grabbed the remote control from the cubby, and pushed the button. The familiarity of the abundant bougainvillea around the gate was comforting. His phone buzzed with a text message. *Zeynep?* It took him a moment to recognize the name. She was asking if he was going to be in Reina again one of these days.

Cenk drove through the open gate as he thought of her in her low-cut peach dress from last night. He pushed the remote control's button again to close the gate. As the two broad pieces of heavy, ornate ironwork closed behind him in his rearview mirror, he texted Zeynep back and said, "Yes. And I'm sorry for leaving early. I'll buy you a drink this time."

Zeynep immediately texted back a thumbs-up and a salsa dancer emoji.

When he reached the door, Cenk opted to ring the bell rather than let himself in. He knew Nazlı *Hanım* would be awake and answer the door. As he waited, he thought of her favorite saying, "The way you arrive is the way people see you."

From the living room, on her iPhone Nazlı *Hanım* watched the video feed from the entrance as Cenk patted his hair down, wiped his eyes, and tucked in his shirt. She couldn't read his expression, but something seemed different about her beloved child. Did he look older? Was he not happy to be back? Had he cried? Or was it the harsh light above the door or the quality of the digital feed, which made him look like something punched him from inside? She couldn't tell and didn't want to think about it further. He was back, and that was all that mattered. She put out her cigarette in a crystal ashtray and ran her hands over the sides of her head to make sure her hair was in place all the way to the top of the bun her stylist had given her that morning. She took a deep breath, walked to the door, and unlocked the bolt.

Cenk straightened at the sound, ready to be seen—and determined not to tell her what happened because he didn't want her to know that she was right.

OUTING

By the time I show up for our weekly outing on Thursday evening in the summer of 2019, my friend Yaprak has already ordered the first bottle of red wine. We're meeting on the patio of Büyük Truva Oteli, one of the oldest and most expensive hotels on the shore of the Dardanelles in downtown Çanakkale in northwestern Turkey.

She beckons me with her left hand to our quiet corner. Her right hand puts out one of the many cigarettes she has already smoked. The night is young, and I've brought two packs of Camels just in case. I'm a little late, and I already know what she'll say.

"Cenk, where the fuck have you been, you *ibne?*" she says and laughs.

Yaprak's the only one who can call me a fag. The only one I'd let.

"Didn't you have enough of your new boyfriend's dick yet?" she whispers. Her whispering is another person's talking.

I look around to see if anyone has heard her. I've tried telling her not to be so loud when she says such things, to no avail.

"Have you had enough of Metin's yet?" I ask.

I've been dating my boyfriend for only two months. She and Metin have been together for almost six.

"Well, his, yes. Dick in general? Hell no," she says and shakes an empty plastic bottle at the waiter for more water.

A few mezes—feta cheese, shepherd's salad, stuffed grape leaves and pepper, moussaka, and sautéed liver—are laid out on the table for our noshing. She pours wine into my glass and drops the bottle into an ice bucket, which is sweating rivulets that seep into the white tablecloth. In the July heat, we like even our red wine cold.

"Trouble in paradise?"

"No, it's just . . . things change, you know."

She's being vague, but I get it. I'm twenty-six, and she's in her forties. Neither of us remembers how many men have passed through our lives, she as a two-time divorcee who dates to find her next husband, and me as a *gey* man who can date but cannot get married. Yet our hearts, encrusted with heartbreak, both real and imagined, still have room for a teenager's excitement about a new beginning and a veteran's hope that it'll be different this time.

"*Siktir et,* let's drink to boyfriends past and present," she says.

Yaprak's cursing like a sailor contrasts with her rather delicate name, which means "leaf." She's the only child of one of Çanakkale's most prominent families—her father is the head of the Chamber of Commerce and her mother's a lawyer—and she's an accomplished architect who is not beholden to anyone, so she can speak her mind. She's what my guy friends and I call *taşaklı kadın,* a woman with balls.

I laugh and raise my glass, "To boyfriends. May we never run out of them."

"*Amin,*" she says, gulps down the last of her wine, and immediately sips from her water. "Drink, drink, drink," she says, gesturing to my sweating glass of water, and gets up. "I've got to pee."

We'll be prodding one another like loving yet annoying mothers throughout the night to drink plenty of water amid the summer heat to avoid massive hangovers in the morning.

This restaurant is one of the best places in Çanakkale to view the sunset. I take it all in: couples strolling arm in arm, parents dragging behind kids preoccupied with Maraş ice cream in one hand and trailing a balloon from the other, and groups of young men smoking or roughhousing on the promenade of the Dardanelles.

On the shore across the strait, the clover-shaped rampart of Kilitbahir Kalesi, an old maritime fortress, dwarfs the apartment buildings surrounding it. To the right of the fortress in the distance are forested hills that overlook the strait. A shaved rectangular portion of one of the hills commemorates the Battle of Gallipoli through the Dur Yolcu Anıtı, the "Stop, Passenger" Monument, which is composed of painted stones that lie on the hillside beneath the Turkish flag—a white star and a crescent moon against red—on a tall pole. The monument would be several stories high if it were vertical. Enormous white stone figures of a red-flamed torch and a soldier with a rifle are stationed next to the first two lines of Necmettin Halil Onan's poem "Bir Yolcuya," "To a Passenger," exhorting passersby, in giant white capital letters, to remember the battle and the lives lost on the Gallipoli peninsula during World War I:

DUR YOLCU! BILMEDEN GELIP BASTIĞIN
BU TOPRAK, BIR DEVRIN BATTIĞI YERDIR.
"STOP, PASSENGER! THIS SOIL YOU STEP ON UNWITTINGLY
IS WHERE AN ENTIRE ERA HAS SUNK."

Farther down the promenade on our side of the strait, the fake behemoth of a Trojan horse built for the Hollywood movie broods as it towers over those strolling by. Hard to believe that Brad Pitt hid in it, and that it came all the way from America. The historic site of Troy is about a half-hour car ride from the city center. Naturally, the downtown Büyük Truva Oteli we're drinking at tonight is pompously named after it: The Big Troy Hotel. Cheap plaster reliefs depicting war scenes with soldiers, horses, and chariots adorn the inside of the building. Ah, the star-crossed lovers: Paris, who abducted Helen, "the face that launched a thousand ships," and Achilles—Brad Pitt—and his male companion Patroclus—Garrett . . . Somebody. And the carnage and heartbreak that ensued. I've seen the film on the Internet.

My gaze shifts to the clientele populating the nearby tables in the garden restaurant: businessmen in suits probably discussing the vagaries of the economy; their sun-kissed wives or mistresses with perfectly coiffed hair and revealing blouses debating the merits of the dishes and the drinks they ordered; and foreign tourists in T-shirts and jeans imbibing *rakı*, indulging in mezes, and taking selfies in the waning sunlight. I wonder if there are any *gey* men in the crowd. Occasional eye contact might offer a clue, but I can't be sure or take the risk of finding out. I'd check Hornet, the app popular since Turkey's Grindr ban a few years ago, on my iPhone, but I've promised Yaprak, and myself, to give my current boyfriend a serious shot. I squash the urge by emptying my wine glass and taking a long drag on my cigarette. The combination of smoke, wine, and heat makes my head spin, so I hydrate. Yaprak would approve.

"*Allah'ım*, we didn't even say a proper *merhaba*! How boy-crazy are we? Come, give me a hug!"

As we embrace, her low-cut orange summer dress, printed with red hibiscuses, shimmers in the sun. She's wearing Ambre Solaire bronzing sunblock with coconut oil. Her hair is in a ponytail, the sides of her head wetted with water to cool down and keep stray hairs in place. And of course, her sunglasses are glued to her face, never to come off until after sunset in the summer. Like she always says, she's a woman of a certain age, so she needs to take care of her skin, especially around the eyes.

"You look great and smell delicious," I say.

"Thank you. So do you. I like that baby beard you got going," she says as she runs her index finger down the side of my face. "How're things? How're you?"

"*Iyiyim*, I just moved to my new office at school, and started reading up on policies and protocols. Necessary evil." After I moved from Istanbul to Çanakkale, I enrolled in a one-year teaching certificate program, which I completed in 2016. I had taught math since, until I decided to transition to school administration.

"Oh yes, Mr. Assistant Principal. Congrats again! *Çin çin.*"

We clink and drink to my promotion.

"How do you like it so far?"

"It's nice. A bigger office with a better view of the schoolyard. It's quiet at the moment, and I'm excited about not teaching for a change. But it'll be crazy soon enough—I need to handle detentions and more parents, of course."

"Ah, parents are the worst," she says and laughs.

"I wish all parents were like you, *canım*. How's Jale?"

Jale, her fourteen-year-old daughter and only child, attends the middle school where I work. She came out as lesbian a few weeks ago.

"She's good. We're learning new things every day."

"Like what?"

"Vocabulary, people, questions. All of it."

"Care to elaborate?" I light a cigarette and pass it to her. I light another for myself.

"Thanks, *şeker.*" She takes a long drag and exhales sideways before she speaks. "She's been staying up late and reading stuff online."

I raise my eyebrows.

"It's not what you think. I'm not spying on her. She told me herself."

"Okay, what did she tell you about?"

"Well, words. Lots of them. When we were growing up, it was just *heteroseksüel*, *transseksüel*, and *homoseksüel*. Now, it's *panseksüel*, *nabinary*, *baç*. Who knows how many more—fuck, I feel like I'm being dragged under by a riptide of words."

"Umm, yeah, I know some of those words. And don't forget *biseksüel*."

"Of course. How could I? When Jale first came out, I thought she was confused or *biseksüel*—I mean she's so young, how could she know for sure?"

"Yes, I remember that. You hoped so, so that she'd have a way out." When I came out as *biseksüel* in my late teens, Nazlı *Hanım*, my mother, was relieved I wasn't *gey*.

She purses her lips. I can't see her eyes behind her shades. For a second, I feel as if Nazlı *Hanım*, whom I left behind in Istanbul, is sitting across from me.

"You know I accept my child and will support her no matter what. I just want her to be happy."

"I know, I know," I say, "I'll drink to that." We drink again. "So, what else have you learned about?"

"One day, I'm a *heteroseksüel*, and the next day, I'm a *sapioseksüel*. Who knew?"

"What?"

"See, even you don't know it. And you call yourself *gey*!"

"Shall I return my *gey* card, *Madam*?"

"It means I'm attracted to intelligence."

"Not to worry then. You're still heterosexual."

She gives me the middle finger and continues, "It's true. I've only married and slept with intelligent guys. *Et kafalılar* turn me off."

"What about Metin?"

Her boyfriend didn't go to college.

"Come on, Cenk, there're plenty of meatheads with college degrees."

True. "Ah, the meatheads, they don't get enough credit either way. They may not be marriage material, but they have a different set of skills. Maybe you shouldn't date to marry for a change?"

"The old me would say I'm too old for that shit, but the new me screams who the hell knows!?"

"I like the new you." I raise my glass, and we drink the remaining wine in our glasses.

She refills us and smokes. She leaves her cigarette in her mouth, wrinkling her nose and squinting, as she says, "I mean how do I know I'm *heteroseksüel*? I might be *biseksüel*. I've married both guys I fell in love with, as soon as they reciprocated. Maybe I've never met the right woman."

"Well, it's not that changeable. I can tell you that. You'd know by now, even if you've never slept with a woman."

"How're you so sure? Is there a test or something that I'm not aware of?"

"Yes, it's called the head-turn test. For me, it's always been about who makes my head turn on the street. That's always been guys. Even when I thought I was bisexual."

"What's your type, again? I forgot how you put it."

"Broad-shouldered and narrow-hipped guys get me going."

"So, a model. Every man's dream, *gey* or straight. How original."

I poke my tongue at her.

"How can you be so sure? You haven't always been with such guys."

"My point exactly. Where're they now?"

She stops for a moment. More wine. "Fine. What do you think about *panseksüellik*?"

"What's that?"

"Your *gey* card, please, *Beyefendi*?" She extends her hand, palm up.

I pretend to get it from my wallet and hand it to her. She throws my imaginary *gey* card over her shoulder toward a table of all-male bankers behind her. The waiter had forgotten to remove the *Rezervasyon*: Akbank sign from the table. One of them looks our way. Did my card hit him?

"Bullseye. I think the cute, tall guy at the table behind you caught it."

She turns around to look as I tell her not to. She turns back and licks her lips.

"Ahem. Now that my uninformed gayness is out of the way, let me guess: *Panseksüel* means someone who likes everyone?"

She giggles. "Let me educate you, Mr. Assistant Principal. One of Jale's friends is *panseksüel* and loves a house. Jale just told me."

"What? You mean like getting off at the thought of a beautiful villa or something?"

"Yes."

"You're joking!"

"No, I'm not. Jale has a lot of *LeGeBeTe* friends, and she told me that one of them is a *panseksüel* in that way."

"Uh, that'd be a fetish. I think they're making a fool out of you."

"Who's being narrow-minded now?" She crosses her arms and raises an eyebrow.

I don't respond immediately. I top off our glasses and empty the bottle. She looks around for the waiter and flags him.

I'm amused and surprised by her confusion. How could an intelligent person who draws plans for the interior of high-rise buildings all over the world for an American firm be so confused about matters of sexuality? Is she, or are we, already drunk? My mind drifts to the world outside Çanakkale; on the fiftieth anniversary of Stonewall in America, Onur Yürüyüşü, the Pride March, is banned in Ankara, Istanbul, Izmir, Antalya, and Mersin. My Twitter doomscrolling tells me that even in America, where same-sex marriage is legal, ignorant, white supremacist *homofobikler* are in power. Yaprak is certainly more open-minded than my mother, who's known about me for a decade. What's the big deal if she's a little confused—and drunk at the moment? I decide to go with the flow and not irritate her further. I make a mental note to look up *panseksüellik* later.

"*Tamam*, I promise to be more open-minded if I can get my *gey* card back."

"You'll get it in the mail in seven to ten business days. Call 1-800-031-6969 to activate when you receive it."

"*Teşekkürler, Madam*. What other words have you learned?"

"*Nabinary*," she says timidly.

"Not male or female?"

"Yes. This is the one that bothers me the most. Jale says that maybe she is *nabinary*."

"So what?"

"If she's not a man or a woman, what is she?"

"*Nabinary*. You need to free your mind." I can't help it.

She grabs the bottle from the metal bucket with a clang, jostling some ice water onto the table, and fills our glasses to the brim. She puts it back with another clang, splashing more water. She takes off her sunglasses and puts them in front of her. The sun has yet to fully set.

"Don't joke. This one hurts my heart." She puts her hand on her bosom and tears up. "We can say *nabinary* back and forth between us, but the world is cruel, and I want my child to be happy." She dabs her eyes with her pink cloth napkin.

"I'm sorry," I say and hold her free hand. "You've been a great mother—a Gezi Park *annesi*. You told me you went all the way to Istanbul for the protests. You've made yourself an activist. How many people are there like you in this country?"

"Please don't call me a Gezi *annesi*. It reminds me of mothers whose children have been injured with tear gas canisters and plastic bullets. Or even killed. And it's gotten worse."

She's right; it's harder than ever to be a *LeGeBeTe* or anyone else who is critical of the state of the country, especially after the coup attempt in the summer of 2016 that, thankfully, failed but made our government increasingly authoritarian.

"Fine, but Jale is lucky to have a mom who accepts and loves her."

"I don't know how to protect her. She wants to go to the Onur Yürüyüşü in Izmir or Istanbul next year. I could take her, but the thought of her experiencing gas and bullets during her first Pride March kills me."

"Don't go until it's safe. Remember I told you what happened at Mekan?" I recall being tear-gassed in that nightclub in Istanbul—the burn in my throat, the tears down my cheeks, and the relief of finally making it outside—with Gökhan, the handsome older guy I had just met. I didn't answer his texts in the aftermath of that scary evening and haven't reached out to him since. He didn't seem to have his life together, especially for someone his age. Ironically, having walked away from the family fortune and its pressures, I'm in a similar position, living in a small apartment and working for a monthly salary.

She nods and sighs. "But really, when is it going to be safe?"

"I don't know, but things will probably get worse before they get better."

"That's what I was thinking, too."

"You've got to tell her that."

"I agree, but just the fact that I need to tell her that hurts."

"*Maalesef.*" I get up, pull my chair next to hers, and sit, putting my arm around her. "I mean what I said: You're doing a lot just by being there for Jale. In the few weeks since she came out, you've come a long way, light-years farther than *my* mother, who keeps quiet and acts like everything is the same." I look away to quell the ache stirring in my chest. "All you can do is be there for her and let her find her way. Like we all had to. You can't control the world."

She nods and kisses me on the cheek, and says, "Call your mother soon."

I give her a hug before returning to my side of the table, and propose a toast, "To mothers like you."

"To friends like you," she says and drinks. "While we're on the subject, Jale has been chatting with Aslı, this older girl, online."

"How much older?"

"Jale says she's sixteen. And she wants to meet her. Cenk, you should talk to Jale."

"What about?"

"Well, you're a normal *gey*, not like my friend Tamer from college."

"Normal *gey*?" I scoff. "What's wrong with Tamer?"

"Nothing, really, he's just very flamboyant and sleeps around. As if that's his life's goal. You know the type. I want Jale to have a more wholesome influence in her life. Not become a barfly."

"Well, minus the flamboyant part, I was once like him. Is that how you would've thought about me if you knew me then?"

"Come on, you and Tamer are not the same."

"*Her neyse.*" There are more important matters than Tamer. "As I told you before, Jale shouldn't know about me yet."

"About that," she says and simpers.

"You told her, didn't you?"

"I had to. And she was so excited about it. If you were in my shoes, you would want her to have someone to talk to, wouldn't you?"

I can't believe she played the mother card. I take a deep breath, rub my face with both hands as if it's the end of a prayer, and exhale. I finish off what remains of yet another glass of wine, despite a sudden wave of nausea.

My head spins as I stumble toward the men's room inside the hotel. I realize the sun has fully set. The night is upon us, and the darkness that drapes the Dardanelles in the distance makes it look like it's been snatched away, leaving an abyss in its place.

As I squeeze out the last few drops of urine, I smolder at Yaprak's reckless behavior. I zip up, wash my hands, and check my hair. I have a short haircut that butches me up. Summer freckles on my face. I see a fledgling pimple on the side of my head. How did I miss it? I feel a pinprick of pain as I squeeze it. It's now a puffy pink spot. I splash my face with cool water.

As I'm about to leave the restroom, one of the Akbank men enters. He looks at me. I nod. He doesn't nod back. Does he know about me? Did he hear us talk? I pull down the collar of my T-shirt with my index finger. The sun might be gone for the night, but it's still hot.

When I step back outdoors, I feel all eyes are on me. I walk through the flotsam of tables carefully to avoid stumbling and drawing more attention to myself. Yaprak is laughing and gesturing as she chats with the tall businessman from the Akbank table. Has she told him about me? I get why her chatting with random men bothers her boyfriend. They stop talking, and she turns back to our table just before I arrive.

"Are you alright? You seem flushed. Drink water."

"Is it that obvious? I just popped a pimple."

"*İğrenç*," she winces.

"I'll tell you what's gross. Your outing me to Jale, a child."

"Come on," she says, "you know her. She looks up to you. And she knows not to tell."

I lean forward and glare at her. "You want me fired?"

"I'll make sure she won't tell anyone."

"Let's hope she's not as trusting of people as you are."

"You've always been like this."

"What do you mean?"

"It's like when we first met. You didn't want anyone to know."

We met during my first parent-child conference at the school. I came out to her soon after we became friends.

"And?"

"It's been *three years*. You still don't want anyone except me and your boyfriend to know?"

"No." I pound the table.

"Calm down. No more wine for you," she says and puts on a smile. *Tencere dibin kara, seninki benden kara*—pot calling the kettle's bottom sooty.

I pour myself another glass of wine. I light a Camel. I make a point of offering her neither. She gives me a sheepish look and fills her own glass. We're determined to drown it all in red.

"Look, I'm sorry," she says. "She won't tell. I promise."

"We'll see. Maybe she already has." I'm determined not to let her off the hook that easy. "And make sure you don't blab about her, either."

"I know how to protect my child. Don't lecture me on parenting."

"I just want to make sure you understand. We're not characters in the Yaprak show of open-mindedness."

"*Siktir git*," she says loudly enough to turn several heads our way. She pushes her chair back and stands up unsteadily.

I've finally gotten a rise out of her, so I pile on. "See, this is what you *heterolar* don't get." I shake my cigarette-holding right hand at her. "You don't walk in *kuir* shoes, so you don't get to tell. Got it?"

She'd storm into the hotel except she's drunk. She turns around slowly and walks as if she is an old lady with leg problems. I don't go after her. For now, I want her to feel bad. When she finally reaches the building, she grabs the arm of the waiter at the door and holds onto it as she speaks to him. It looks like she needs support to stand up, but I know her. I bet she ordered another bottle of red.

While Yaprak pouts in the restroom, I pull out my iPhone and call her boyfriend, Metin.

"Who's this?" says an unfamiliar voice on the other end.

Shit, I misdialed. It's the other Metin, the school janitor, in my contacts. I saved his number for building-related emergencies.

"I'm sorry, I dialed the wrong number," I say, trying not to slur my words.

He hangs up without saying anything. Fortunately, he doesn't have my number yet.

The waiter brings a bottle of Kavaklıdere Yakut. Yaprak is definitely coming back.

I squint at my phone as if I'm nearsighted or really old and can barely pick out the names. I navigate to the two Metins in my contacts. No last names. I tap each with my fingertip to view their numbers. Not that I memorized them. Who does that these days? Metin the janitor lives near the school, and I know my work area code, so I call the other one.

"*Nooldu?*" he says. No greeting, no warmth, no nothing. He's always like that with me, as if I'm not man enough for him.

"Yaprak," I say and can't find the words, like I'm intimidated by him all of a sudden.

"Is she okay?"

I hear music and people talking loudly in the background.

"She's okay. Where are you?"

"Eceabat."

A half-hour ferry ride away, on the other side of the Dardanelles. He lives there, born and raised, and owns a furniture store. They met when Yaprak was doing pro bono consulting for a family friend there. I don't know what Yaprak sees in him. He doesn't have a college degree, and he is a typical man in the way he neglects her.

"What're you up to?" I ask.

"Hanging out. Entertaining some guests."

"Anyone I know?"

"You don't know them. Why's she not calling me herself? Put her on."

Bossy. Maybe that's what she likes about him. That, or he has a big dick. Which he does. She told me herself.

"She's just drunk and in the restroom. You know how she gets."

"Of course, what else," he mutters.

Maybe there really is trouble in paradise.

"Can you come get her?"

"At this hour? Not sure. And my guests."

"We argued a little."

He ignores that bit of information because he knows how we get when we drink together.

"Hold on, I'm checking the summer ferry schedule."

He won't make it. I already knew that.

"It's past midnight. I missed it. The next one is at 2:00 a.m.," he says.

"No worries. I'll see what I can do. I'll text you if we need you. *Görüşürüz.*"

I see that Yaprak is on her way back. As she approaches, I tally the signs of drunkenness. Her face is flushed, her hair is somewhat disheveled, even though she probably put in some effort to keep it together, and one of the spaghetti straps of her orange dress has fallen below her shoulder.

"Who were you talking to?"

"Metin."

"Why, did he call you?

"No, I called him."

"Why?"

"Well, you're too drunk, and as your boyfriend, he should come and take care of you."

"What the fuck, Cenk?"

"What?" I feign ignorance.

"You know." She holds her forehead like she's received news of death. Dramatic.

"Why are you coming between me and my boyfriend?" she asks.

"I'm not."

"Yes, you are. He doesn't want me to drink, and you call him and tell him that I'm drunk."

"Well, I didn't know that."

"Now you do. Stay the fuck out of my relationship." She's ready to pounce on me like a lioness.

We are quiet for a minute and drink from the Yakut I've poured for both of us.

"I know what you're doing," she says. "You're still mad at me, so you step over me and call my boyfriend."

That's exactly it. "I don't know where you're getting that."

"*Allah kahretsin*, stop playing games!" She's the one pounding the table this time. Her other strap falls. I reach out to pull it over her shoulder. She cringes and slaps my hand. "Don't touch me."

"*Tamam, tamam*, I'm sorry," I say, "I'm just drunk."

She leans back and takes a deep breath. "Have I ever come between you and your boyfriends? Did I call Alpay when he was fucking around behind your back, and you knew it?"

"What does he have to do with this?" I ask. We're experts at pushing each other's buttons.

"It wasn't easy for me to see you being disrespected, but I've never disrespected you. I expect the same."

She literally held my hand through that debacle and many others since.

"I said I'm sorry. What else do you want me to do?"

"Call Metin back and tell him that I don't need him. Now."

I dial Metin and am about to tell him exactly that when the sleepy and angry voice of the school janitor says, "Brother, you misdialed again. Stop calling me!" He hangs up.

I start giggling and almost fall off my chair.

"What's so funny?" says Yaprak.

"Hold on, I'll tell you. Let me call your Metin first."

"My Metin?"

I hold my index finger up at her as I dial Metin. I tell him we don't need him and Yaprak sends her love.

He says, *"Tamam,"* and hangs up.

I tell Yaprak about misdialing the janitor twice. I get the giggles again, which makes Yaprak smile in spite of herself. Her smile is encouraging. Maybe she'll forgive me. I get up and put my arm around her. She doesn't move, except for turning her head sideways and offering me her cheek. I give her a peck on the cheek. As I move back to my seat, my head is spinning.

We avoid eye contact and don't say anything for several minutes. The late-night sea breeze exhales through the emptying patio.

I rub my eyes and say, "We shouldn't have ordered this last bottle. It's so late. And I have a morning meeting."

"You can leave," she says. "I want to stay a bit more and finish the Yakut."

She's still sore from our altercation. I am, too, and it doesn't feel right to leave her drinking alone, but I need to go home. "Are you sure?"

"Yes," she says, "I'll take a cab."

We both took the bus here today so that we could drink as much as we wanted.

"Call me if you need me."

"I will." She doesn't get up, so I go to her, kiss her on the cheek again, and say *hoşça kal.*

As I stumble out of the restaurant and shuffle through the hotel, I fumble for my wallet and apartment keys to make sure I have them. I hail a cab at the front entrance.

Once on my way, I sit back and enjoy the cool night breeze caressing my face and gliding through my hair.

Then I remember my mental note about looking up *panseksüellik.* I Google it: "Pansexuality, or omnisexuality, is the sexual, romantic, or emotional attraction toward people regardless of their sex or gender identity."

Interesting. I return my iPhone to my pocket and lean back. My mind drifts to Yaprak and myself: when we first met—I was a new transplant to Çanakkale so that I could be myself, and she was a recent divorcee getting back to dating yet again—and we were trying to figure each other out. When I came out to her, we became closer. And now, we continue supporting each other in whatever imperfect ways we can. She's family to me in a way no one else is.

I pull out my phone and text her that I'll speak with Jale, followed by two emojis: a heart and a hug. I add the Wikipedia link to my favorites; it could be handy when I talk to Jale.

When I arrive at my apartment, I take off my clothes and set my alarm so that I can wake up and check on Yaprak in an hour. Just as I'm falling asleep, I hear the faint ping of an arriving text. I squint at my phone and make out her text: "*Teşekkürler*, I knew you would!" followed by her signature trio of emojis, which I cherish: a rock star, a middle finger, and a kiss.

INGÉNUE

t's a quiet Friday evening in the fall of 2019, and I'm at my retired baba's apartment. I visit him once a week for some father-son time. I bring him groceries and sometimes take him to doctor's appointments. He's seventy and has high blood pressure and aching joints.

Tonight, I have an additional, important reason to visit: *Benim Çocuğum, My Child*, a 2013 documentary by Can Candan about the organization LISTAG, the Families and Friends of LGBTIs, and their meetings and activism in Istanbul. It features parents who have come to accept their children—it took one parent ten years.

When Baba found out I was *gey* from my late mother, who had found activist pamphlets in my backpack, he looked for someone to blame. First it was my mother for letting me hang around women when I was young, then himself for not spending enough time with me, and finally me and my friends for encouraging one another's "vices." This was fifteen years ago when I lived in Bağcılar, Istanbul. I'm forty-three now and have moved a few times since, widening the geographical, as well as metaphorical, distance between us. I finally settled in Antalya, where I work as a tour guide. After my mother's passing last year, and with my sisters married and busy with their own lives, Baba followed other military retirees and moved from our old town of Çorlu in the northwest a few months ago to be near me in this city with mild winters in southwestern Turkey on the Mediterranean Sea.

We see each other often but don't talk about my sexuality. Given Baba's health, we might not have much time, so I gave him the DVD a month ago—now it was his move. *Tek başına oyun olmaz*—one cannot dance on one's own. He texted early this week and said that he had watched the film, so I expect we'll talk about it.

As a warm-up to our conversation, we're watching *Küçük Beyin Kısmeti—The Young Gentleman's Destiny*—on TRT 2, a state television channel no one watches anymore, except for old folks like Baba when it's showing classic Turkish movies. The 1963 black-and-white Yeşilçam movie features late Ayhan Işık, the heartthrob leading man of the time with a Clark Gable moustache, and voluptuous brunette Türkan Şoray, one of the enduring stars of Turkish cinema and my baba's favorite actress. It's a comedy about two young people who've never met but have been betrothed to each other by their rich, businessman fathers. When Şoray's character appears in disguise as a nerdy girl, no more the ingénue she was at the beginning of the film, I know that she is about to teach a lesson to Işık's womanizer. I've seen enough of these movies to make an educated guess.

During the commercial break, I go to the kitchen to replenish our teas and text my boyfriend, Hasan: "We're watching *Küçük Beyin Kısmeti* on TRT."

"I know every line of that film, Gökhan! I was nerdy Şoray one time," he texts.

Hasan, my *aşkım*, my beloved, is as *kuir* as they come. He makes his living as a drag queen on weekends at the Sinema *gey* club. He also works as a male belly dancer during the week in the pricy Liman Kafe & Restoran in Kaleiçi, the historic city center dating back to the Roman Empire. Tour guides like me take tourists there regularly.

When I first saw him there, I thought he looked familiar, but as soon as he started dancing, his sinuous body moving in a two-piece belly dancer's costume, his chest with trimmed hair shimmying almost made me forget who or where I was. At the end of his entrancing performance, he walked from table to table and collected tips. When he came up to me, I tipped him generously as he stared at me like he saw a ghost from the past. Looking into his green eyes up-close confirmed that he was indeed Hasan, my best friend from high school who disappeared one summer and didn't return at the beginning of the following school year. When I asked his parents at the time, they said they didn't have a son anymore.

I didn't speak with Hasan immediately. We were both on the job, so I thought I should respect his privacy around strangers, plus I had to take my tour group back to their hotel. Lost in the glow of his performance, I wondered as I drove at his transformation from the quiet teenage boy I'd known at school back in the day to the man who now was in charge in his enthrallment of all sorts of people, including me, who sought entertainment in his illusion. Knowing that he recognized me, I returned to the restaurant alone and asked him out for a drink when his shift was over.

I took Hasan to the Marina Teras Restoran with outside seating that overlooked the harbor where yachts and boats were docked. It was early fall and still warm, and we both wore T-shirts and jeans. As soon as we ordered our food—a fried fish with a side salad for him, a hamburger and fries for me, and beers for both—I peppered him with questions. I hadn't seen him for more than twenty-five years.

"What happened to you? How did you end up here? I mean, I'm glad you did." I hoped my eagerness wasn't intrusive.

He took a deep breath and exhaled. "My parents couldn't stand having a *kuir* son, so they tried to fix me by sending me to the Koran school. I refused to go that summer, so they beat me." His expression betrayed a familiar vulnerability followed by a certain hardness I didn't recognize.

"So, that's why you disappeared. I'm sorry. Minus the beating, my parents'—I should say my father's—reactions were similar."

"How did they find out?"

"My mother went through my bag while I was visiting. I had started volunteering for Lambda Istanbul. Not knowing what to do, she told my father."

"Were you angry at her?"

"I was hurt, but not angry. My mother's world was small, and she didn't know any better. And she's gone now, so none of that matters anymore. I know she loved me; she told me so the last time I visited her in the hospital."

"*Başın sağ olsun,*" said Hasan to convey his condolences.

"*Teşekkürler.*"

"Glad you could have some sort of closure with your mother."

"Me, too," I said.

The boats in the harbor gently rocked to the ripples and the wind.

"What about boyfriends?" said Hasan.

"There've been a few. I was with Cengiz, my college roommate, for a while, but he moved abroad. And I had one right before my mother outed me to my dad, but it didn't work out," I said. "Ateş loved drama too much, so we weren't a match. What about you?" My life had been a story of no matches.

"So, he was a drama queen. Well, I'm a drag queen," said Hasan and pointed at himself. "I do a drag show a couple of nights a week at Sinema. You should stop by."

Fascinated, I said, "I'd love to."

"About boyfriends, flings here and there. Nothing serious. You know how men are," said Hasan.

I thought there had to be more to it, but I decided not to pry. He scratched between his middle and wedding fingers of his left hand, which reminded me of the surgery he had when we were kids in Çorlu.

"How's your hand?" I asked.

"It's fine. Botched but fully healed," said Hasan as he held it out for me to examine it.

A strip of pale white skin with creases stretched from the top of his hand through his wedding and middle fingers to his palm. The excess flesh and skin, the so-called webbing, were carved out of the base of those fingers, and his hand still carried the scars and stitch marks.

I put my other hand over his and said, "I'm sorry you went through that. It seems so unnecessary."

Hasan pulled back his hand gently and said, "Tell that to my parents."

"Have you talked with them since you left?"

He broke eye contact with me and said, "No. And they've never tried to find me."

As he looked toward the harbor with a blank expression, I remembered avoiding him at school toward the end, right before he left, so I said, "I owe you an apology for my behavior at school. I think I knew we were both *gey*, but I worried being around you would out me. That was cruel, and I am really sorry."

Hasan looked at me and said, "Apology accepted, *canım*, but save it for the marriage proposal. And yes, you were distant, but you learned your lesson, didn't you?"

I nodded, knowing he was referring to how that *izbandut* Atilla pushed me into the water during a school trip and how Hasan had warned me before that to be careful around him and his posse.

Hasan continued, "It was so obvious you liked Mert—hey, every-one liked him—so I get it, but you should see him now. According to Facebook, he's married with two kids, complete with a dad bod and bald head. Who's looking better now?" He mock-flicked his hair, straightened in his seat, and crossed his legs.

Encouraged by his comment, I gave him a once-over, followed by a thumbs-up and a wink.

At the end of the meal, I asked Hasan to go home with me. To my delight, he agreed. Before we left the café terrace, I threw my arm around his shoulder, looked around to make sure we were alone, and kissed him on the lips.

At my apartment, we listened to old Madonna and George Michael songs and reminisced about the old days until we went to bed. We didn't have sex that first night; instead, he opened up to me about how he had done sex work in Izmir before he moved to Antalya and became a performer. He also told me that he was *pozitif.* I told him that I had met many people who did sex work or had HIV when I volunteered at Lambda Istanbul, and that it was okay, that he was okay. I could see him truly relax for the first time since we reconnected, and him being himself reminded me of when we were young and innocent.

For the rest of that night, we lay next to each other, talked about other things we'd never told anyone else, and held hands until we fell asleep. We dated for a few months before I asked Hasan to move in, and I promised not to let him down ever again.

It's Turkish cinema night at the club. Every Friday, Hasan dons the drag of a different actress and works the club, providing campy commentary as the audience drinks and watches classic films, and lip-synching and dancing to musical numbers. Out of drag, he's slim and wears his dirty blond hair with a few gray flecks in a short bowl cut with bangs over his forehead, plucked eyebrows, and soulful green eyes that melt my heart whenever he looks at me. In drag, and at the age of forty-one, his transformation is close to magic; he could pass for a woman.

Hasan had told me earlier in the day that they'd be showing a Şoray movie tonight: *Dünyanın En Güzel Kadını—The Most Beautiful Woman of the World*—a 1968 melodrama about a poor female singer and a rich man who fall for each other.

"How're the patrons liking the movie?" I text.

"You know how it goes, Gökhan. They watch it when she sings and dances," texts Hasan.

"Of course. Have you done the Tamba Tumba Esmer Bomba dance yet?"

Later in the film, Şoray's character dances in a tight blouse and capri pants and sings the famous "Brunette Bombshell" song.

"Not yet, but I hope I can find my balls after these pants! Why did I do this when I had several other, more comfortable options?"

Şoray dons quite a few costumes in that movie, dressing up as a belly-dancing concubine and a gypsy girl and cross-dressing as an Ottoman gentleman, as well as wearing several couture gowns.

"I'm sure you will, *canım*—however squished they might be."

Hasan laughs at my message and changes the subject, "So, have you talked with your baba yet?"

"Not yet. After the movie," I text.

"You can do it, *canım*. I believe in you," texts Hasan.

Hasan has wanted to meet Baba since Baba moved to Antalya. I gave him the runaround until he asked, "Are you ashamed of me?" I said no, and that's the truth; it's more like Baba and I have unfinished business, plus being *gey* around Baba is embarrassing because he asks about sex, like who is the "man" and who is the "woman," as if that's what intimacy is all about. Or, sometimes, he acts like other men, strangers, who'd rather pretend *LeGeBeTe'ler* don't exist. I didn't want to lose Hasan, so I promised him I'd introduce them after Baba watched the documentary. They can meet if our conversation goes well.

After I text, "*Teşekkürler, canım*," I return to the living room with our teas.

Baba's living room has a beige sofa that faces the TV, with a walnut coffee table in between over a large carpet with blue and gold arabesque. There are two armchairs with a swirling floral pattern, one on each side of the sofa.

My mother watches us from the framed black-and-white picture on the wall, taken at her and Baba's civil ceremony. He's in a suit and smiling broadly. She's wearing a dress, not a wedding gown, and her smile is barely there. They had to get married because she got pregnant with my older sister. I wonder how she would've reacted to my life with Hasan and what's happening tonight. I suspect she would've liked him, and they'd get along well. She didn't meet him or his parents but knew about him as my best friend when we were at school. After I told her how he'd disappeared, she brought him up from time to time, asking if he was found and praying that he was well wherever he was.

Another frame contains one of my drawings, a family portrait. When I was young, Baba used to take me to work at the military headquarters. I'd sit at an empty office desk, drawing Baba, myself, my two sisters, and *anne*, always with that same half-smile from the photograph. It warms my heart that despite everything, Baba kept this drawing and had it framed.

Baba is laughing at the TV and thumbing the beads on his *tesbih*. He carries his rosary with him everywhere, now that he is old and has gotten religious, "preparing himself for the inevitable," as he reminds me from time to time. He worked as an officer in the army for forty years. As a government employee, he has always supported the ruling party, a continued habit despite retirement, so he now votes for Adalet ve Kalkınma Partisi, the religious right, by default. I disagree with his politics, which is one of the reasons I'm nervous about the possibility of him meeting Hasan.

"Who were you texting, Gökhan?" says Baba. I guess I took a bit longer in the kitchen.

"Hasan," I say. He's never set eyes on Hasan, but he knows we live together.

"Am I going to meet Hasan?" says Baba.

"You can," I say, "but we need to talk first."

When the Şoray movie ends, Baba turns off the TV. I move from one of the armchairs to the sofa, where Baba sits. I put my iPhone on the coffee table and ask, "When did you watch the documentary?"

"The next day."

"Why didn't you tell me?"

"It was difficult to watch. You know, mothers crying, and even fathers were tearing up." He looks down and fiddles with his *tesbih*. His balding pate, covered with white hair silky as a baby's, shines in the fluorescent light from the ceiling in his living room.

I get impatient and ask, "So, what do you think?" I brace myself for whatever is coming.

"The parents seemed normal."

"*Evet?*"

"Like they could be my friends or neighbors."

"*Evet.*"

"Especially the *babalar.*"

"That's why I wanted you to watch it."

"Did you know that there's a group for families in Antalya called Akdeniz Aileleri?"

The Mediterranean Families? "Really? How did you find out?" I would never expect Baba to be the one to inform me about a local organization.

"I read about it in *Körfez.* I went to their meeting Tuesday evening." I'm speechless.

"Guess who I met there?" says Baba. The wry smile on his face shows his eagerness to share more—or gossip.

"Who?" What else is he going to pull out of the bag?

"Remember Tuncay *Bey*?"

"Tuncay *Amca* from your work? *Harbiden*?"

When I visited Baba's work as a child, Tuncay *Amca* always gave me pocket money to buy chewing gum or chocolate at the canteen. His wife, Zehra *Teyze*, was friends with my mother, and they would talk on the phone when Tuncay *Amca* and Baba were out drinking after work.

"*Evet.* They live in Antalya now, since Tuncay has retired from the army. He's the one who recommended Antalya as a city for retirees."

"What was Tuncay *Amca* doing there?"

Baba raises his bushy eyebrows and looks at me like I'm being deliberately obtuse.

I think of their son who was a shy kid with curly hair and chubby cheeks. "How's Olcay?"

"Olcay wasn't there. Tuncay told me that Olcay is a girl."

"Olcay is trans?" I ask.

Baba nods. "I think so. But Olcay still likes women like a man does. How did Tuncay put it?" He scratches his scalp. "*Trans lezbiyen.* Olcay has a girlfriend."

"*Allah'ım*, we haven't seen each other since high school."

"Tuncay asked about you. I told him you were *gey*. I thought you wouldn't mind."

"I'm fine with it, if you are," I say, feeling a warmth spread from my rib cage toward my throat. I'd normally suppress the emotion, but this time, I let it be. It makes me tear up. I rub my eyes once as if it's because of dust.

"I didn't know what else to say about you."

My tears recede, and I blurt, "What did you expect? You refused to know me all these years."

Baba remains quiet. An acknowledgement of remorse?

I don't know what gets into me. I let it all out, "Remember you said it was a sin, that a man like you could never have a son like me. And my mother, she didn't know any better, but your refusal of me silenced her forever. She had to walk on eggshells around you until her last moment, when she told me on her deathbed that she loved me no matter what." At this point, my tears flood back, and I'm crying full-on, with sobs, snot, and all that, which are dousing my anger. My outburst at him feels both embarrassing and righteous.

Baba passes me his checkered cloth handkerchief, like the ones my mother used to iron and fold after laundry, and says, "I'll give you a moment," and walks out of the living room.

I wipe my eyes, blow my nose, and take deep breaths.

When Baba comes back in five minutes, his eyes are puffy. He gives me a hug. When we're both seated and collected, he says, "I'm sorry, *oğlum*. If I could turn back time, I would. All I ask now is that you let me make it up to you, for your mother's memory at the very least. She asked that I reconnect with you before she passed away. And I'm trying."

I nod and say, "You can tell Tuncay *Amca* that I live with my boyfriend, Hasan, when you go back." I feel relief.

"Tell me more about Hasan," he says.

I tell him how we met, what he does, and how long we've lived together. He nods and listens. When I'm finished, he says, "I didn't know you had a friend named Hasan in high school. It must be kismet that brought you two back together after so many years. I want to meet him."

"He's wanted to meet you for a while now."

"Invite him over," says Baba.

"Now? Are you sure?"

"Yes," he says and turns on the TV. "Let's see what's next."

I text Hasan, "Baba and I just talked. I told him everything about us, and he wants to meet you—*tonight*."

"What, just like that?" texts Hasan. "I mean, the mere mention of my name does tend to have a powerful effect on people who have yet to meet me, but really, how did that happen?"

"After he watched the DVD I'd given him, he attended a local parents' meeting—he read an article about it."

"A budding *kuir* activist!" texts Hasan, followed by a flamenco dancer emoji.

"I guess. There was some yelling and ugly crying, too. I'll tell you about that later. When can you be here?"

"The movie just ended. I'm changing now."

I see three moving dots. Hasan types, "I have a thought. What if I showed up in drag?"

I hesitate. The last time he was in public in drag, a couple of men called him *dönme*, turncoat, on the *dolmuş*. He told them to *siktir*, and one of them hit him. The driver threatened to call the police, which would've made things worse for Hasan, but fortunately, the men left the bus, still swearing at him. He came home with his left eye swollen shut. After that, we agreed that Hasan wouldn't go around in public in drag. The *cinsiyet* war on those who are different rages on.

"*Alo*?" he texts.

"What did we agree last time?"

"Don't worry. Koray will drop me off."

Koray, the handsome bartender, is a good guy.

I write, "As crazy as it sounds, it's kind of perfect because you are in Şoray drag, and she's Baba's favorite."

"And yours," replies Hasan. "Actually, all Turkish men love her, no?"

"Yes, especially the older gays."

"So, that's a yes?"

I hold off texting for a few seconds. Are we really doing this? I love Hasan as he is, with everything he is, so I text a thumbs up.

"By the way," says Hasan, "I won't be in capri pants with boobs up to my face. I'll wear something more classic, more glamorous. Şoray as a rich bitch."

"Baba won't know what hit him!"

If anyone can pull off the big-eyed, long-lashed, button-nosed, and luscious-lipped brunette diva of Turkish cinema in the best way possible, it's Hasan.

I tell Baba, "Hasan should be here in half an hour. What's on?"

"*Selvi Boylum, Al Yazmalım* will start soon," says Baba.

The Girl with the Red Scarf is a timeless love story directed by the auteur Atıf Yılmaz in 1977. It's acclaimed as one of his and Şoray's best movies—and as one of the all-time classics of Turkish cinema.

I replenish our teas and settle in to watch the film with Baba. If only he knew what is afoot. I wipe my eyes one more time with the sleeves of my T-shirt, rub my clammy hands on my pants, and sip my tea. I feel the warm beverage trickle through my gullet and briefly drown the butterflies in my stomach.

An hour after Hasan's last text, the doorbell rings. Baba attempts to get up, but I tell him not to worry, that I'll get it. He has changed into a white short-sleeved shirt and brown slacks, his usual outfit for entertaining guests.

I open the door and stare at Hasan. Voluminous black hair cascades just below his bare shoulders, and he has long eyelashes with mascara; thin bow-shaped eyebrows; powder-white skin; and red, pouty lips, complete with Şoray's trademark mole on the right cheek. He's given her iconic look a modern twist: he's wearing a strapless black gown with a sequined rainbow around the bust and huge rainbow-colored peace-sign earrings framing his face.

All I can manage to say is, "How was the drive?"

"Good," he says and waltzes in.

We hug after I close the door. Holding him in my arms feels good; he smells like peaches and cigarettes. He gives me a peck on the lips. Fortunately, we're in the foyer, and Baba is still in the living room. Hasan mimes for me to wipe the lipstick he left on my lips. I rub my mouth with the back of my hand.

"Don't you have anything to say about my *balıketi* realness?" he whispers.

We watch *RuPaul's Drag Race* on the Internet.

I whisper back, "Is this Şoray as *gey* Audrey Hepburn? I'm not sure it's historically accurate."

"Audrey was a global icon. You should be thankful that I'm not Şoray as a villager in drop-crotch print *şalvar* pants, a handknit cardigan, and a headscarf. You know, before she moves to Istanbul and marries rich."

True. I can't help but crack a smile. "Funny you say that, because we're watching *The Girl with the Red Scarf*, and she's wearing a *şalvar*."

"Ah, she doesn't marry rich, but I still love that movie, especially the scene when her mother rubs soot on her face so that men won't notice her," says Hasan.

"Yes, that makes Baba laugh every time," I say.

Unsure of what to do next, I freeze. Hasan pats me on the back, takes off and slings his long black gloves on the back of the chair in the foyer, hooks off his stilettos with his index finger, and kicks them under the chair. He pats his wig down, takes a deep breath, and strides into the living room where Baba is, as if onstage. I follow like I'm in a dream.

The next thing I see is Baba looking our way, frozen in the motion of lowering the volume. He drops the remote, which hits the floor with a loud thud; its back opens and two batteries roll out.

I scurry and kneel to pick it up and put the batteries in, snapping the lid back on. He stands up. I leave the remote on the coffee table.

"*Merhaba, amca,*" Hasan says and takes Baba's right hand, which he seems to have forgotten to extend as the elders usually do.

Baba swallows and looks at me like he has seen a ghost, as Hasan kisses the top of his hand and touches it to his forehead.

"*Merhaba . . . kızım . . .* I mean, *oğlum . . . hoş geldin,*" says Baba. He doesn't sit until Hasan settles into the other end of the sofa.

I sit across from them on the edge of one of the armchairs.

"My apologies, *amca,* for disturbing your peace this late," says Hasan.

Baba clears his throat and says, "*Sorun değil,* we were just watching a movie." He gestures to the TV and sips from his tea.

The Girl with the Red Scarf is about Ilyas, a truck driver, and Asya, a poor villager, who fall in love and elope before Ilyas leaves Şoray's Asya for another woman. After looking and waiting for Ilyas to no avail, Asya marries another man who is good to her. Kadir İnanır, the dreamboat of '70s Turkish cinema, plays Ilyas, who returns to Şoray's Asya; they still love each other, but it's too late.

We're quiet in front of the television for a couple of minutes. Ilyas and Asya are eloping in his truck named *Aldırma Gönül,* "Don't Worry, My Heart," which he speaks to and confides in as if it were a family member for some reason. Asya was to enter into an arranged marriage if she were to stay, so they announce their forbidden love to the trees, rivers, and cows as they drive.

Baba clears his throat and says, "Gökhan tells me you're coming from work."

"Yes, I'm an entertainer at a local club," says Hasan. "We have a show where I impersonate film stars as we screen their famous movies. Among others, I do Türkan Şoray."

"Like Huysuz Virjin?" says Baba, referring to Seyfi Dursunoğlu, Turkey's one and only drag star, whose stage name means "Crabby Virgin."

"Exactly," says Hasan and smiles.

"I've been a fan of Şoray for many years. I've seen all of her movies and TV shows," says Baba and adds, "You even have the mole."

"Türkan Şoray is happy to meet you," says Hasan and, without missing a beat, adds, "Gökhan should bring you to our show."

I mumble, "Perhaps. If Baba wants."

Baba nods slowly but doesn't say anything. There's a slight crease between his eyebrows. He's probably wondering how a man can be made to look like his favorite star.

"Ouch!" says Hasan, pointing at the screen.

Baba and I turn to the TV and see that it's the scene where Ilyas slaps Asya. After helping Cemşit, a driver whose van broke on the side of the road during a storm, Ilyas gets demoted from driving his beloved truck to being a mechanic. Without Ilyas's knowledge, Asya talks to his boss to save his job, which upsets Ilyas.

"Why do men jump to conclusions so fast, *amca*?" says Hasan. He feigns ignorance like one of those ingénues Şoray has played countless times on the widescreen.

"Well, *namus* is important, you know," says Baba.

Baba is talking about honor, which makes men do all sorts of horrible things to others, especially women.

"Whatever it is, I hope it is for the best of their relationship," says Hasan, switching to Şoray as damsel in distress.

Baba glances at me with a quizzical expression, then looks at Hasan and says, "*Inşallah, kızım*—I mean, *oğlum*."

As if neither knows how the movie ends.

I reflect on how Baba addressed him. *God willing, my daughter.* And then the immediate correction: *My son.* Is this really happening?

Baba continues, "This is the scene that rattled *rahmetli* the most. Asya doesn't deserve it. One should never raise a hand at a woman."

Rahmetli? "I didn't know my mother liked this movie," I say. What else do I not know about her? A familiar feeling of grief, from my earlier outburst, returns and envelops me.

"Not only that, she would speak back to the television and yell at Ilyas when he cheated on Asya and acted stupid, like in this scene. *Nur içinde yatsın,*" Baba says and sighs.

"*Nur içinde yatsın,*" repeats Hasan.

I glance at the framed picture on the wall and mouth the same blessing. May she sleep in divine light.

A commercial for Algida ice cream puts an end to our commemorative digression.

Baba says, "Gökhan, why don't you make more *çay?*"

Hasan nods and looks at me. "Gökhan, I brought some *kuruyemiş.* Why don't you get it from my bag and pour some for us?"

As I get up to leave the living room, I contemplate Hasan's strategic choice. Nuts mixed with pumpkin and sunflower seeds, all roasted, are Baba's favorite.

"I'll make the tea," says Hasan.

Baba says, "*Yavrum,* don't wear yourself out. Gökhan can make it." The old affectionately call the young *yavrum*—my darling.

Çay is Baba's other addiction. His friends call him *teneke boğazlı* for a reason. He is a fast drinker of hot tea, as if his throat is tinned.

"It's no trouble, and my tea is better than Gökhan's," says Hasan. He winks at me while Baba turns to the TV, and follows me to the kitchen.

I feel Baba staring at our backs. I wonder what he thinks about Hasan.

As I pour *kuruyemiş* into small, heart-shaped ceramic bowls in the kitchen, Hasan pinches my butt. When I protest that Baba might see us, he pinches the other cheek. He puts the kettle on the gas burner. As we wait for the water to boil, he checks to make sure his chest and hip padding are in place. He looks for the *çay* next and finds a rotting chicken sandwich in the lower cabinet. He clutches his chest and pretends to suppress a scream and then grabs it with a napkin and throws it into the trash bin under the sink.

"We should check all the cabinets. First thing in the morning. This place needs a woman's touch," he says to me as if he is my wife.

I'm simultaneously embarrassed, worried about Baba's forgetfulness, and amused.

Hasan's next discovery is a jar of old, almost empty *mesir macunu*, a traditional, sweet and spicy Turkish paste that is thought to impart health and strength. Many believe it's an aphrodisiac. He raises his left eyebrow, curls the right side of his red-lipped mouth, and says, "It looks like Baba is getting some."

I put my index finger to my lips and say, "Throw it in the trash. It's probably moldy, and Baba is too old for that kind of stuff." My view of the kitchen has shifted. It looks untidy and worn out, and Hasan is right, it's in dire need of tidying up.

He finally locates a package of *Çaykur* and infuses two tablespoons of black tea leaves in hot water. We return to the living room, Hasan carrying a metal tray with the *kuruyemiş* and three narrow-waisted *çay* glasses and me holding the kettle. He places the tray on the coffee table, and I pour and serve the tea. Hasan hands out two small bowls per person, one with *kuruyemiş* and another for the husks.

We separate kernels from husks and eat peanuts and pumpkin and sunflower seeds, punctuated with sips of hot black tea, with sugar for me and Baba and no sugar for Hasan, who is always cutting carbs. The black tea keeps us awake despite it being past midnight. The *kuruyemiş*, lots of it, saves us from further awkward conversations and helps us focus on the drama unfolding on television.

After leaving Asya, Ilyas moves in with Dilek, the woman who manages the drivers' schedules at the office. Meanwhile, Asya meets Cemşit, the van driver Ilyas helped; Cemşit takes her and her young child in, but Asya still loves Ilyas.

"Cemşit is such a good man," says Hasan.

Baba nods and says, "Ilyas is young and stupid. Cemşit is mature and dependable and knows loss. He's what Asya and her son need."

I think of us losing my mother to cancer, and the time Baba and I lost when we became distant after he found out that I was *gey*. I look at Hasan and then Baba, and my heart is full.

"Men," says Hasan and sighs. "Why can't a woman have both passionate love and stability?"

Baba glances at Hasan.

"What's your favorite scene?" I ask them.

Baba says, "It's coming now. When Samet, Asya's son, calls Cemşit *baba*. A child needs his baba, and that scene never fails to turn the faucet on."

Baba does indeed wipe his eyes when the time comes.

When the scene passes, I turn to Baba and say, "My favorite is when Ilyas has an accident and Cemşit, Asya's new husband, brings him home. Samet, who is Asya's son with Ilyas, calls Ilyas *amca*, uncle, instead of *baba*."

"That's another heartbreaker," says Hasan.

"Indeed," says Baba, "That's the moment Ilyas learns his lesson, but it's too late."

When the scene comes on, we all repeat in unison what Ilyas says, "*Kimim ben bu evde? Neyim?*"—Who am I in this house? What am I?—and laugh.

"Baba looks at us and says, "Very *felsefi*. This is why this movie is so good."

"Finally, a man asks the question women grapple with all their lives," says Hasan.

"What's your favorite?" says Baba to Hasan. His interest in him melts my heart.

"Besides the soot-on-the-face scene, it's the tragic ending, when she reflects on love," says Hasan.

"That's a good one, too," says Baba.

When that scene arrives, we're all ears and eyes. Ilyas takes Samet for a ride and contemplates kidnapping him. When Samet cries, he pulls over. Samet runs to Cemşit, who has been looking for them. Upon her arrival at the scene, Asya must choose between Ilyas and her son and husband. Her voiceover says, "*Sevgi neydi? Sevgi iyilikti, dostluktu, sevgi emekti*"—What is love? Love is goodness, friendship, and labor. Close-ups of Ilyas and Asya alternate; they still love each other, but the child seals the choice. The end.

By now, we're all full and tired. Baba turns off the TV and says, "They made the right choice. A child's happiness is the most important thing for a parent. Let's go to bed and get some rest."

He retires to his room after telling me to sleep on the couch in the living room and to put up Hasan in my old room. According to tradition, couples cannot sleep in the same bed at their parents' until after they get married.

I take Hasan to my room. We shut the door, which has honeycomb-patterned, opaque glass inset in its upper half, and hug and have a proper kiss finally. We laugh and help one another wipe smudges of lipstick afterward.

"That wasn't so bad, was it?" asks Hasan.

"Well, we're both still here."

"I think he likes me. He even gets what I do. He did mention Huysuz Virjin."

"I know. Why didn't I tell him that before?"

"Because, at forty-three, you clearly still have *baba korkusu*," he says and taps my chest gently. He's right about the "fear of the father," the proverbial Turkish concept of respect mixed with fear that kids are brought up to feel before their fathers.

"You should've seen us earlier. I basically told him that he and I could've reconnected years ago, when my mother was alive, if he accepted me."

"Ouch—and good."

"We both cried. I needed to say my piece for a change. Anyway, I'm glad he has finally met you," I say and hold his hand.

"Me, too," says Hasan.

We're both quiet, processing this moment.

"It feels nice to have you here in this room—Baba decorated it like it's my room," I say.

"I feel like I'm getting immersed in your childhood," says Hasan. He walks up to the framed pictures of me as a baby and a young boy, on the wall above my old desk. He runs his fingers over a few toy racecars with chipped paint, and he kneels by the side of the bed and looks at the covers of several old issues of *Araba*, a magazine about sports cars, piled on the floor.

"Feel free to browse them if you have trouble falling asleep. I have extra pajamas in the dresser."

"Are you trying to butch me up? I'm into boys who like cars, not cars."

"You got me there."

We hug and kiss again one more time, in quiet celebration of tonight.

Through the glass in the bedroom door, we see the light in the hallway turn on. We catch a glimpse of an opaque image of Baba fluttering by toward the bathroom.

"I'd better go," I whisper, "Make yourself comfortable. Feel free to use the bathroom off the foyer to take off your makeup. *Seni seviyorum.*"

"*Tamam.* Love you back. *Iyi geceler,*" says Hasan.

I close the door, tiptoe to the living room, and lie down on my makeshift bed on the couch. I hear the sound of the faucet in the kitchen and watch Baba enter the living room holding two tumblers full of water. He brings one to me, like he always does when he comes to my bedroom to say goodnight on the occasional nights I stay here.

Illuminated by the faint streetlight that seeps in through the curtains, he says, "I'm glad to have met Hasan."

I say, "He feels the same. Thank you for welcoming him here."

He pats my head and says, "*Iyi geceler.*"

After he leaves, I can't help but replay the details of the night. I'm certain I won't be able to fall asleep.

Baba gently shakes me awake in the morning. He has opened the curtains, and sunshine floods the living room.

"Put on your clothes. Let's go for a walk." He usually walks before breakfast.

I rub my eyes and look in the direction of my room. My neck is stiff.

"Let Hasan sleep," he says as he walks slowly toward the door. "We'll just walk a few blocks to the park."

I put on my sneakers and follow him. The cool morning air licks my face, but the first ray of the unforgiving Mediterranean sun flicks the coolness away. It's a quiet Saturday morning on Piri Reis Caddesi, the street that leads to the seaside Atatürk Parkı. A few kids are playing on the shady side of the sidewalk, and a young man is returning home with freshly baked bread from the neighborhood *fırın*.

Baba rents in Bahçelievler, the "Houses with Gardens" neighborhood of central Antalya, in an old housing development of eight six-floor apartment buildings near the beautiful public park that overlooks the Mediterranean. He cannot afford the newly built or renovated apartments in this area. The weathered facade renders the cluster of buildings where he lives out of place amid the new construction.

Atatürk Parkı is only a few minutes away across Konyaaltı Caddesi. When we cross the boulevard and enter the park, Baba says, "It was *fantastik* to meet Hasan as Türkan Şoray right when we were watching her most famous movie."

"When I told him you knew what he does, he wanted to come as her in drag," I say. "I was worried."

"How else could I meet Şoray?" says Baba. "Does Hasan wear men's clothes?"

"Yes, when he's not working."

"But perhaps he's trans?"

"Just because he's *gey* and does drag doesn't mean he's a woman."

"I see," Baba says and adds, "Either way, Allah must've created him that way."

I nod and blink to squash a tear.

"I hope you see what I'm trying to tell you," he says and pats me on the back.

"I do, Baba. *Teşekkürler.*"

We sit quietly for a bit. I notice we're on a commemorative park bench. I touch the gold plaque engraved with the name of a dead man. I look at the life buzzing around us and the deep sea with darkening shades of navy blue in the distance. *Katır tırnağı*—mule's hoof, the ubiquitous local succulent vine—drapes over the rocks and hangs down the nearby cliff like a green crochet, dotted with pink flowers with yellow centers. I hear the waves crash against the rocks and into the caves below. The sound reminds me of our summer outings to the beach when I was a child. Baba would swim to deep waters, and I'd sit with my mother and sisters on the sand and watch him in the distance, until he swam back to us on the shore.

Baba slaps his thighs to signal that it's time to go back. As I help him up, he says, "Did you give Hasan pajamas to wear?"

"I did."

"Will he be Şoray when we're back?"

"No. Drag requires a lot of work, and he needs a break before tonight."

"*Tamam*, whatever is comfortable. He's my guest."

We leave the park the same way we entered on Konyaaltı Caddesi. After we cross the street, Baba says, "Text Hasan to put the kettle on. We'll buy a few *poğaca* on the way. What does he like? Feta cheese, olives, or potatoes?"

"He likes the potato pastry," I say as I pull out my phone to text him.

When we get back home, Hasan, out of drag and in my spare set of blue gingham pajamas, opens the door and welcomes us inside.

"Hasan *oğlum, günaydın,*" says Baba as he enters.

Hasan *my son, good morning.*

I reach down and exhale as I untie my shoes. When I step into the foyer, the old pinwheel-shaped rug my mother knit hugs my soles.

ACKNOWLEDGMENTS

As an English major at Boğaziçi University in Istanbul in the mid-1990s, I took a short-story course with Oya Başak. Her larger-than-life personality and enthusiastic instruction made this small-town kid fall in love with the genre.

While my enjoyment of short fiction dates back to the previous century, my daring to write stories—and queer ones at that—is more recent. I've regularly taught two survey courses, LGBTQ+ Literature and The Short Story, at UConn's Stamford campus since 2008. The productive overlap between my teaching and writing at UConn enabled me to imagine and eventually write this book. As I tell my students often, writers are readers first, and reading can both inspire you to write and teach you how to do it.

I appreciate my UConn colleagues Sean Forbes and Kathy Knapp, who provided feedback on an early draft of "Sweet Tooth," the eponymous first story I wrote, and Pam Bedore, Pamela Brown, Fred Roden, and Ingrid Semaan for their enthusiasm about the book as I worked on it.

I workshopped several stories in this book with Zaina Arafat and Scott Alexander Hess at the Gotham Writers Workshop and Alexander Chee at the Bread Loaf Writers' Conference. A few fellow writers from the workshop and I formed a writing group, which initially included Ava Robinson, Caroline Shifke, Elizabeth Yerkes, and Ryan Brower and later expanded with the additions of Kathleen Fletcher, Kirk German, and Lila Flavin. I'm grateful for their astute feedback, kind encouragement, and friendship.

I fondly remember the Lambda Literary Writers Retreat for Emerging LGBTQ Voices in August 2018, which provided a much-needed community of fellow LGBTQ+ writers.

Versions of the following stories included in this book were published in literary magazines: "Webbed," *Chelsea Station* (July 2018), reprinted in *Emerge: 2018 Lambda Fellows Anthology* (2019); "Big Sister," *Ploughshares* 45, no. 1 (Spring 2019); "Kastro," *Epiphany*'s Spring/Summer 2020 "The Borders Issue"; "Sweet Tooth," *Joyland* (July 2020); "Outing," *X-R-A-Y Literary Magazine* (March 2022); "Runway," *Iowa Review* 51, no. 3/52, no. 1 (Summer 2022); and "Pride," in *Ploughshares* 48, no. 4 (Winter 2022–2023).

I thank Lisa Williams, the editor of the University Press of Kentucky New Poetry and Prose Series, for selecting this book, and the Press team, including Patrick D. O'Dowd, Jackie Wilson, Ila R. McEntire, and Erin L. Holman, for publishing it.

Many others have shaped this writer and thus helped birth this book:

My family and friends, through their love and faith in me and through the perseverance I inherited from my parents and grandparents, which is invaluable for a writer.

Turkey and the United States, two beautiful countries with complicated pasts and presents; my binational queer existence has inspired and informed this book.

Jeremy Lang Hall, my spouse, who read every story in this book many times; I wish a trusted, intelligent, and loving reader with a sense of humor like him for all who dare to write. I love you.

And Leonardo, my beloved feline companion whose grooming, slow-blinking, purring presence fittingly blessed the writing of this book, this labor of love.